DOUBT

Among Us Trilogy book 1

ANNE-RAE VASQUEZ

Developmental Editor
JOSEFINA ROSADO

Editor
DANKLERR BENADAM

Augmented Reality
PUBLISHING

This is a work of fiction. The events and characters described here are purely fictional and in no way represent or resemble real life events, places or people.

a Truth Seekers end of the world religious thriller

Among Us Trilogy. Copyright © 2013 by AR Publishing, Anne-Rae Vasquez

www.amongus.ca www.anne-raevasquez.com

Developmental Editor: Josefina Rosado

Editors: Danklerr Benadam and Candace Sinclair, WordsRU

Proofing Editor: B. Miller

Cover graphic design by AR Publishing

ISBN 978-0986492136 AR Publishing

✻ Created with Vellum

For Joseph, whose vision and support inspired me to write this book. For my kids, who inspired me to learn about the hidden talents of online gamers. For Kathleen, who pushed the boundaries of my imagination. And for Josefina, who helped me bring Harry, Kerim, and Cristal to life. Finally, for the Truth Seekers who dared to believe.

In loving memory of Manny and Dee who are with us in spirit.

"Doubt is well written with great imagery and some plot twists that I never saw coming. There aren't many books that have such a unique plot twist. Once religion is brought into Doubt, the book gets a little weird but when the pieces start falling into place it making sense. When the background stories of some of the para-normal creatures come to light, the book gets even better. There were two thing about Doubt that I didn't enjoy but the book was so awesome that it was easy to overlook." - *April Gilly, Readers' Favorite Book Awards*

"...As a big fan of the TV show *Fringe*, this book appealed to me tremendously. The writing was well done, and the way the 'supernatural' forces were introduced was great. The characters, primarily Harry and Cristal, were developed and built up very well, and had enough detail about their lives for us readers to understand them as people, not just characters. Genuinely looking forward to reading the rest of the series when it comes out!" – *Melissa Greenberg, Amazon review*

"'How was he going to convince online gamers to leave the privacy of their virtual world to work with others in the real world?' is the question that ends chapter three. As someone who is married to an online gamer, that strikes me as a really good question. You don't have to be a gamer or know one to identify with the characters. I would definitely recommend it to a friend and I'm really looking forward to the second book." – *Ginger Lego, Amazon review*

"*Doubt, Among Us Trilogy*, by Anne-Rae Vasquez, was a good and refreshing read for me. I am not too into books about the supernatural, but the idea of gamers on assignments was intriguing. The author uses this story to show that we are spiritual in nature, either for good or for bad. I would recommend this book to a friend. I will read book two and three because of the interesting way the subject of angels and demons is approached. A good, clean read for any age." – *S. Coleman, Goodreads review*

"I like books that go straight to the point without a flood of unnecessary introductory words. And this one grabbed me from the beginning with the idea of time travel... The author's style is light and pleasant to read and I read it very quickly. And when thing got more complicated I couldn't stop reading." – *R. Chelebieva, GoodReads review*

Dear Truth Seeker,

I believe in capturing history and this is my attempt to leave our story for the future generation of Truth Seekers like you.

I have asked all my Truth Seekers to keep a journal. I encourage each one to write their thoughts, events, and ideas so as to preserve the story as close to the real events, thoughts, and feelings as possible. I want history to remember us not just from my words but also from the words of my closest and dearest friends—even friends who have ended being my worst enemies.

Your mission is to share these events with other Truth Seekers. Keep the faith that "Good" will prevail. We must stay united in mind and in actions. We must maintain our perseverance to save humanity and the world.

Harry Doubt
Truth Seekers Unite!

PART I
SEEKING THE TRUTH

One step at a time
The water feels fine
Think I'll wade in some more

AR Vasquez

CHAPTER 1
NEW YORK 2008 - HARRY

C OINCIDENCE? HARRY'S MOTHER always told him that there were no such things as coincidences. Only fools believed in that garbage.

This may explain her erratic behavior when his father, Aaron Doub, a respected quantum physicist, collapsed in front of them. A simple, impromptu, after-work dinner party, which his mother Bina was hosting at their home, had turned into an unforgettable nightmare.

His father's last words were, "We have the theoretical and experimental capabilities to build a time machine to the future. We have also discovered a scientifically feasible way to go back into the past..."

He remembered how his father's marble brown eyes bulged out of their sockets; his mouth opened as if to finish the sentence. Then, in slow motion, Aaron fell forward, his face landing into the pile of whipped mashed potatoes on his plate in front of him. The glaring bald spot, which Aaron meticulously polished and combed over every morning, was all that Harry could see from his end of the table.

What would Dad do if he had built his time machine earlier? Would he be here right now?

Harry glanced over his shoulder wondering if there was the slightest possibility that an 'Aaron Doub from the past' was standing in the shadows, observing the circus freak show unfolding at this particular point in time.

His father's colleague, Dr. Saeed Nariman, also a quantum physicist, lifted his father's head from the plate while another guest helped wipe the mashed potatoes from his father's face. They both lifted his father and placed him on the floor. In a daze, Harry stood up and walked towards his father's inert body.

His mother was on the other side, waving her arms in the air, and wailing at the top of her lungs, "They killed him! They killed him!" she cried.

Who killed him? Harry thought.

Thankfully, a wife of one of his father's colleagues came and guided his mother away. Harry stood motionless, watching in awe as Dr. Saeed placed his mouth on his father's lips. Aaron's chest rose up and down with every breath Dr. Saeed blew into his mouth.

Dr. Saeed glanced up at Harry and glared at him, saying, "Don't just stand there, Harry! Call 9-1-1!"

❦

HIS FATHER WAS PRONOUNCED dead an hour after they arrived at the hospital. Harry was walking back from the vending machine. The ER doctor came out of surgery and found his mother and Dr. Saeed in the waiting room. Harry could read from the grim expression on the doctor's face that the news was going to break his mother's heart.

"We found a small clot lodged in your husband's brain," the

doctor said to his mother. "It caused hemorrhagic damage to the surrounding tissue. I'm sorry, Ms. Schwartz...we did all we could."

His mother, Bina, pushed the doctor away, screaming, "No! It's not true!"

The doctor waved to a nearby nurse who went to get help. His mother stepped forward and grabbed the doctor's scrubs with both hands.

"He's not dead! What did you do to my Aaron?"

When he didn't respond, she turned wildly towards the other people in the waiting room, and pleaded, "They took my husband! Please help me!"

Harry wasn't surprised with her reaction. She was an Israeli wife and mother who tended to be over dramatic when she expressed her emotions. But something in her eyes made him wonder if she was right.

Three nurses came rushing back, grabbing hold of his mother's arms.

"Let me go! Let me go!" she wailed, as one of the nurses stabbed a needle into her arm.

"You need to relax, Bina," Dr. Saeed said in a soothing tone.

He helped guide Harry's mother down into a chair.

"Everything will be just fine," he told her.

"Saeed, you need to find Aaron," his mother said, before passing out.

Harry had observed everything from a distance; not fully comprehending what was happening.

Funny how a tiny blood clot could bring a man as brilliant as Aaron Doub to his demise.

❦

HARRY WAS ONLY seventeen when his father died; a university senior writing his thesis, *Mind-Reading Computers: Intelligent Assumptions of Complex Thought Processes.*

Besides the fact that his father was an atheist and that his mother pretended to be one too, growing up in Harry's home had been anything but normal. The rare times Aaron was home, Harry might as well have been invisible.

Sometimes his father would notice Harry in the room, turn and ask his mother, "Is the boy studying his Hebrew? He must never forget our heritage. We are Israelis first, Americans second."

Then he would rattle on and on about his theories, asking Harry what his opinion was on the matter. If Harry even tried to respond, eight times out of ten, his father would spin around and say, "Where is Saeed? You're not Saeed!"

When Aaron did not confuse him with Dr. Saeed, Harry could actually have a profound conversation with his father. But those moments were so infrequent that Harry had to mentally accept the fact that he didn't really have a father.

Now that Aaron was dead, Harry didn't have to pretend anymore. A year later, Harry legally changed his last name to "Doubt."

CHAPTER 2
BINA SCHWARTZ - HARRY'S MOTHER

F our years later, Harry was feeling optimistic about the future. He was in his room at his desk, staring at his laptop, re-reading an email that was open on his screen. He had read it so many times that he knew it by heart.

Dear Harry,

Although you will be receiving the official documents from our legal department, I wanted to write to you personally to say that it was a pleasure meeting you. We at Google Inc. are delighted to acquire the rights to your Truth Seekers online game. The legal documents and bank draft have been sent to your home address.
Please reconsider the job offer as we could use someone like you on our team. Feel free to swing by Google Inc. headquarters the next time you are in California.

Sergey Brin
Co-founder, Google Inc.

HARRY SMILED as he picked up the courier box from his desk. His mother poked her head in the doorway.

"Dinner is ready, Harry," she said, eying the box. "Is that what you've been waiting for all day today?"

"Yes, Mom," he said. "It's finally here."

He ripped open the top and took out a thin binder of documents. He reached in again and pulled out an envelope.

"You never told me how much money you sold the Truth Seekers game for. Like I always say, 'a mother understands what a child does not say.' You know you created that game when you were only eight years old. I hope you didn't just give it away to those Google schmucks," she said as she walked up to him.

She frowned, placing her hands on her hips. Harry stifled a chuckle. What could he say? She was just being who she was—an overprotective mother.

Harry tore open the envelope and pulled out the bank draft; the smile on his face stretched wider.

"Harry, did you hear what I said?" Bina asked, raising an eyebrow, her patience coming to an end.

He waved the bank draft in her face. Bina squinted her eyes to read what was on it.

"Is this a joke, Harrell?"

She often referred to his legal birth name when she wanted a serious answer from him.

"No joke, Mom," Harry said. He leaped up, grabbed her around the waist and gave her a big hug. "Our money worries are over!"

She nodded her head in support but the frown remained on her face.

"But Harry, this Truth Seekers' game is your baby. How could you sell it for that *pitsvinik*? It's not enough!"

Here we go again.

"Mom, are you kidding me? That's a ten-digit figure. What do you mean it's not enough?"

She took a deep breath and said, "So my brilliant son thinks ten digits is enough. Why not twenty digits? Thirty? Your game is your life. You know this is true!"

Harry put his arms around his mother's waist, planting kisses on her cheeks. She pretended to push him away, but he knew she enjoyed the attention he was giving her.

"Stop it, Harry. That's enough."

He stepped back and shrugged, hiding his smile from her.

"Okay, if you say so."

"Oh? You stop so easy? Harrell, don't you love your mother?"

Her eyes were wide with surprise.

Harry laughed and gave her an enormous bear hug.

"Don't worry, Mom. Google didn't buy the rights to the Truth Seekers' name. I already made a better Truth Seekers game and brought it underground. It's hosted on multiple private servers. I call it the 'interranet.'"

Bina gave him a warm smile and pinched Harry on the cheek.

"Ah, my wonderful boy. Your father would have been so proud."

Harry rolled his eyes, and said, "Yeah, whatever, Mom." He bent over and gave her another kiss on the cheek. "Please don't ruin my mood by bringing up Dad again, okay?"

She pressed her lips together, holding back what she was going to say.

"Mom, I'm starving. Something smells real good in the kitchen."

Bina raised her hand.

"Wait, Harry. I wanted to tell you this at dinner, but it is better if I tell you now."

"Okay," he said. "What is it?"

"I decided I am going to Global Nation in Tel Aviv. I want to be a peacekeeper in Gaza while the peace talks between Israel and the Palestinian Authority are happening," Bina said.

Harry's eyes widened.

"Are you crazy, Mom? Why do you want to go there? You and Dad came here to New York to get away from all the politics and now you want to go back?"

"I have to go, Harry. I need a purpose in life," she said, as her voice broke.

He looked at her for a long time, his anger diminishing.

"Are you sure you can take care of yourself, Mom?" he asked.

She smiled.

"I took care of you and your father. *Makhshava me tumtemet le-gamrei*. What a stupid question."

❧

TWO MONTHS LATER, Harry received a phone call.

"Mr. Doub, you are listed as the emergency contact for Bina Schwartz. We regret to inform you that Ms. Schwartz did not report to work two days ago at our Gaza office. We are doing our best to locate her and are working closely with Israeli officials to find her."

"I'm coming right now to help find her," he said.

"Be assured we are using all our resources to locate her. We advise you to not come," the official sounding voice said.

Harry decided that his mission was to find his missing mother even if it meant that he had to infiltrate Global Nation from the inside to do it.

CHAPTER 3
GLOBAL NATION 2012 * HARRY

A NEW STATUS ALERT BOX popped up on the bottom corner of his computer screen displaying a familiar avatar—a dark shadow of mist in the silhouette of a woman standing tall, hands on her hips with her long hair blowing wildly over one shoulder like black flames. Cristal aka *Mist*.

Harry, who was known as *Zero*, made sure that the closest members of his team contacted him via the private Truth Seekers' game messaging system. He had overridden the personnel spy software, which the president of GN, Shelley Lionheart, had ordered his team to install on all GN desktops and laptops. Even though he was confident that no one could hack into his system, he made sure that everyone messaged each other using alias names and coded phrases.

Mist: Received the latest mission you sent. Not sure why we need *Shadow* to be involved. His programming skills suck.

Harry smiled as he typed his reply.

Zero: Your comment is noted. Bring *Onyx* with you to location.
Mist: You chose her as a recruit without my input. Take care of her yourself.

Harry began typing a response. He could have easily walked five cubicles down to talk to Cristal in person, instead of texting her via her online alias *Mist*. Her recent snide remarks about his latest recruits, Kerim and Joanna, needed to be dealt with.

Harry had warned Cristal that upcoming missions would become more dangerous. His warnings, however, fell on deaf ears and he feared her cockiness would get her in trouble. So without her knowledge, he had hired former Turkish Army Intelligence Kerim Ilgaz, giving him the alias name *Shadow*, and assigning him as Cristal's bodyguard. If she knew the real reason behind Kerim's role in the Truth Seekers, she probably would never speak to Harry again.

As for Joanna, alias *Onyx*, he couldn't understand what was Cristal's gripe with her. Although Joanna was a good programmer and gamer, having one of the highest scores in the Truth Seekers' game, she lacked the ability to see the big picture—a talent and skill that he found only in Cristal. He never revealed his true feelings to Cristal convincing himself it was a conflict of interest to favor her over the others. After all, he was the head of the Truth Seekers and also technically her boss at GN.

Deep down inside he knew Cristal was the only one who could see through him, past his self-confidence and bravado. Sometimes text messaging was an easier form of communication so he could avoid looking into those kohl brown eyes with flecks of gold, like lasers that could detect his deepest and darkest fears. They were good friends and he wanted their relationship to stay that way.

Mist: I'll meet you after work to discuss this further.

HE SAW her through the glass doors when a gust of wind blew her long brown hair away from her oval face revealing her lips like pink petals, her blue jeans hugging her curves.

When Harry invited Cristal to join the Truth Seekers, she gave up her scholarship at MIT and transferred to Global Nation University. Both of them had been fifteen years old and the youngest students in GN's history to attend the university. Now at twenty-two, they still felt out of place being the youngest staff working at Global Nation.

"Coffee shop is too busy and we really need to focus," he said.

"Okay, so where do you want to go?"

Cristal glanced at her watch.

"Thought we could go to my place," he said, keeping his voice steady.

She raised an eyebrow but then grinned, and said, "Yeah, sure. I'll be the first Truth Seeker to get to see *Zero* Doubt's new crib."

He laughed.

"Just don't post that on the website, okay?"

"Too late, I already tweeted everyone, posted it on Facebook, and all the gaming blogs," she said with her usual snappy retort.

A group of GN staff exited from the building and walked past them, chatting amongst themselves.

Cristal grabbed his arm and said, "Let's go."

She pulled him towards the bus loop.

"Afraid to bump into Joanna? You guys can't just get along?" he asked.

She rolled her eyes.

"Come on, Harry. I have better things to think about right now. Like, why you want me to hack into Shelley Lionheart's private folder on the GN cloud network?"

He turned away from her and sighed.

"You know, I can't tell you that. Your job is to complete your mission and not ask questions, right?"

"Yes, Mr. Doubt," she said, her sarcasm seeping between the words. "So sorry...I forgot that you're all work and no play."

LATER THAT EVENING, CRISTAL AND HARRY were sitting at his dining table with their laptops set up in front of them. Cristal was busy scribbling notes on her pad of paper.

"You have the best laptop money can buy and you're writing on paper," he said, shaking his head.

"Writing with pen and paper helps me brainstorm."

She frowned as she concentrated on her scribbles.

All Harry wanted to do was touch the strands of hair that fell seductively on her porcelain cheek. He watched as she snapped a barrette on the wavy locks against her face.

"Geez, my hair is driving me nuts. One day, I'll lose my patience and shave it all off," she mumbled under her breath.

Harry stared at her in disbelief.

"You don't mean that, right?"

She made a face and said, "Long hair is just a pain to keep up. It would be much easier if I cropped it really short, like yours. Don't you think?"

She put both her hands under her chin, gave him an innocent smile and blinked her eyes.

He chuckled to himself.

"What's so funny, Harry? You don't think I'd do it?" she teased.

She punched him playfully on the arm.

"Wouldn't make a difference to me if you shaved it all off," he said, shrugging his shoulder.

"Oh, whatever, Harry. I can't figure you out sometimes."

From his peripheral view, he could see her sulking in her cute way, her lips in a pout and her eyebrows furrowed together.

Global Nation was behind the disappearance of his mother Bina Schwartz. A conglomerate non-profit organization with offices and universities all over the world, he had enough data to prove that GN hid behind its peace, educational and social activism initiatives to do experiments on innocent people. He needed more data to find out where his mother was and why GN kidnapped her.

Romance was not on his agenda. There were more pressing things at hand.

Focus on the mission, he scolded himself. He didn't have time to be distracted by anyone. Not even Cristal.

৩৬৩

EIGHT MONTHS EARLIER, Harry had put his first mission into motion: landing a job at Global Nation's head office. It was a simple plan and easy enough to pull off by himself. After all, getting his PhD before his twentieth birthday meant that all the biggest companies were lining up and offering him dream jobs with six-figure salaries.

It must have come as a surprise to them, when he applied for and accepted a low-paying job working as a middle manager at the GN central IT department.

"Don't you think you're a little overqualified for this position? The pay isn't even half of what Google was probably offering you," George Beaver had asked him during his interview.

His first impression of the Beav' was that he looked like a potato-head Elf—his huge bald head balancing on top of his short, stocky body.

It was obvious that Beaver didn't understand most of the technical terminology he was reading from the interview questionnaire, mispronouncing terms such as *GUI interface*. In the IT world, it was pronounced "gooey" not "G.U.I."

"I never really had a real job before, so I think I have to earn my stripes like everybody else."

Harry cleared his throat hoping that he had responded in a

humble tone. He would bet his last dollar the Beav' had a Napoleon complex.

The answer must have satisfied Beaver, because he smiled and wrote a few notes on the paper. Then he asked Harry a few more questions and finally he stood up.

"Wait here a moment, Harry," Beaver said, grabbing his papers.

"No problem."

Harry took a deep breath and fixed his tie as he waited. A suit and tie guy, he definitely was not.

Minutes later, the door opened and to Harry's surprise, Shelley Lionheart entered the room. Stylish, in a manly way, she carried herself like an Amazon queen. She was someone who would stand out in a crowd. She was in her mid-forties, wearing a fitted matte black jacket and pantsuit; her raven black hair cut short close to her scalp; blue-black nail polish and lips painted with a dark burgundy color, which contrasted against her dark chocolate skin, and slanted cat-like eyes that seemed to glow like coal-hot embers. On top of all this, at six feet tall, 200 pounds of muscle, she was definitely not one to joke around with.

Quickly, he stood up and stretched out his hand, ready to shake hers. The night before, he had repeatedly practiced in front of the full-length mirrors in his bedroom. A confident handshake is a good first impression, his mom had always told him.

Lionheart looked him square in the eye and squeezed the circulation from his hand.

Satisfied by his lack of response, she turned to Beaver. Beaver quickly pulled back the chair.

"This is Shelley Lionheart, President of Global Nation and GN University," Beaver stammered.

Harry waited to see if he would pull out a trumpet to herald her regal presence.

Lionheart sat down gracefully despite her size, almost as if she was floating into the seat.

Harry pulled back his hand quickly and sat back down.

"Nice to meet you, Ms. Lionheart," he said, trying hard not to let his voice waver.

She folded her hands on the table and leaned slightly towards him.

"Let's get to business. We have GN offices in every continent. We need someone like you to help set up the security firewall for our networks and database servers globally. We had, what we call, an incident at our GN charitable office in Manila, Philippines. Long story short: The web servers were compromised and we experienced breaches in security after the recent riots. The breach involved unauthorized access to personal data of a number of our very important charitable donors. As you can see, this is a delicate matter, which needs to be resolved immediately. Beaver will arrange for you to fly out tomorrow."

She attempted to smile, but the expression on her face resembled someone who had just taken a bite into a bad burrito.

"I haven't been offered the job yet," he said quietly.

"Don't be cute. Or maybe I won't offer you anything, Mr. Doubt." The glimpse of a smile disappeared from her mouth, as she continued, "We both know this job was yours before you walked in the door. The interview was just a legal formality. As you know, we are a non-profit charitable organization. And our GN universities are funded partly by the state with some funds coming from tuitions and fees. Of course, you already knew this, being the recipient of this generosity. We count on our generous donors to help run our charitable and educational operations. So, yes, it's not a glamorous job and probably the pay won't be as attractive as what the private sector can offer you, but at least you'll get to travel. Or, perhaps, you can call it payback. Consider that a fringe benefit."

Harry tried not to smirk.

"Before I accept...when I reviewed the current support model you have now for IT, it is no wonder that GN offices are experiencing security breaches in their networks. GN doesn't have a dedicated IT operations team, despite having multiple offices and universities all over the world. Without the proper security systems in place with regular maintenance and upgrades to the firewalls, it is not a shock that the breach didn't happen sooner. So, Ms. Lionheart, before I can accept, I'll need you to provide me with the best team of programmers to be able to do my job," he replied, trying not to sound too cocky.

The grimace reappeared on her face, as she said, "Call me Shelley. No need for formalities. We're all one family here."

Beaver nodded his head like a bobble-head doll.

"Yes, one happy family," he said.

Beaver started to say more when Lionheart raised her hand.

She tilted her head slightly and said, "Okay, that is a fair observation. What you propose is exactly what we need here. If you take the job, you can hire three people for your team." She paused for a moment. "By the way, you seemed to have impressed George Beaver in your interview. Lucky for you that he will be your senior manager, and you are to report to him directly."

Beaver said with disdain in his voice, "We normally don't offer positions right after the interview. Now you want to create three more staff positions out of thin air? I guess that you must think you're really somebody special."

Beaver looked over at Lionheart and stopped smiling when he met her glare.

Harry almost laughed. Lionheart put Beaver's panties in a wad with one look. Classic.

Lionheart continued, "We checked your references, Harry. Your professors all gave you shining recommendations. It seems that your father's genius has rubbed off on you."

Her eyes seemed to drill into his.

He wasn't sure if this was a compliment or her way of testing him. *It's now or never.*

He took a deep breath and finally said, "My last request is that you let me be the one to interview and hire the programmers for my team. I need the best of the best, and since I'm responsible for this team's success, I want to be the one to choose who we hire."

Beaver glowered at him and turned to Lionheart to see her reaction. She was expressionless, which to Harry was a good thing. It meant that she was considering his request.

"The sacrificial lamb, so to speak," she mumbled to herself.

Lionheart drummed her nails on the table.

After an uncomfortable silence, she said, "Very well, then. You will get to hire who you want for your team."

She waved to Beaver to get up.

"We have concluded this conversation. Beaver will get HR to get your paperwork in order and arrange for your plane ticket. Make sure you check into our health services office to get your vaccinations and meds in order before you fly. We don't want our shining new Manager of IT Operations to get sick on his first assignment."

She stood up and walked out of the room, or to be accurate, she levitated out of her chair and glided out of the room. *Very strange woman,* Harry thought to himself.

"Let's go, Harry. There's a lot of stuff you have to do to get ready for your trip," Beaver said in a bossy tone.

Harry followed him out of the room.

Mission one accomplished. The next challenge was bringing in online gamers to join him on his crusade. How was he going to convince online gamers to leave the privacy of their virtual world to work with others in the real world?

CHAPTER 4
CRISTAL (ALIAS MIST)

W hen Harry recruited Kerim Ilgaz without asking Cristal, she was "nice." She had voiced her concerns about Kerim's technical skills that were not up to par with the others on the Elite team.

"There are other talents we need, not just programming or gaming ones," he said.

Harry didn't share what kind of talents, so she respectfully kept her mouth shut.

And wasn't she *nice* when Harry recruited Angelica? Again, despite her not even being in the top 500 of the Truth Seekers' game, she agreed to train her.

"She will be a significant asset for us when we need it," he assured her.

Serena, on the other hand, was someone she could trust. Stationed in the Philippines, which was twelve hours ahead of New York time, Serena often video chatted with her late at night or early in the morning, all without complaint.

Joanna Chan, on the other hand, was nothing more than a ladder-climbing fraud. During the online game missions, she always broke the rules. One time she led the team into enemy territory with not enough weapons or ammunition despite Cristal's warnings. Although they did succeed in destroying the enemy's munitions building, it was at the expense of losing three members of their team.

❧

TEN YEARS AGO, Cristal Hernandez started playing the online game, Truth Seekers to escape her real life where she didn't fit in with anything or anybody.

She enjoyed losing herself in the fantasy world where the problems of her life didn't matter. She was very aware of things that made her different from other children. Her father called it her special "abilities."

She was able to open a book and read it from beginning to end in a matter of minutes. Words used to lift off the page and flood into her head in waves of sentences, phrases, and paragraphs. Consuming a book was how she used to describe it.

In first grade, her father didn't let her mother buy her dolls or toys. Instead, she received thick computer programming books.

"Programming skills will be useful in the future," he told her.

"Let her be a girl," her mother would say.

Cristal enjoyed consuming the books and sought for more challenging projects, building online applications and web tools and sharing them on GitHub, a web developer's open source community and platform. The power of creating something out of physically nothing tantalized her curiosity.

"Dad, I want to do more projects. What else can you teach me?" she begged him.

"You were meant to do special things, Cristal," he said.

But one day, everything changed.

On her tenth birthday, her father never made it home from work.

She sat on the front steps and waited. Her mother sent home the two girlfriends from school.

Her mom reported him officially missing, filing a missing person report forty-eight hours later.

"He can't be gone, Mom! He just can't!"

She ran into her room and slammed the door. Her heart was racing, her lungs expanding as if drawing in all the air around her, and the room began spinning counter clockwise. The floor shifted beneath her feet and then the walls started to shake.

"Cristal! Stop!"

"Dad?"

She whirled around. No one was in the room but her. The room stopped shaking, her books strewn on the floor, evidence that the event happened. Had her father not called out to her, who knows what damage she could have caused?

After that night, she was convinced she would be reunited with her father one day.

When the police closed the missing person's file a year later, her mother became ghost-like—floating around the house, wordless; an empty vessel.

Cristal had no choice but to fend for both of them. It would have been what her father would have wanted. She made sure her mom made it to her psychiatric appointments and the Help Group at the local church. She learned how to buy the groceries and cook. All the while, she never gave up the hope of seeing her father again. Even if she had wanted to forget, her dreams wouldn't let her.

Her father is standing at a distance, surrounded by a light mist, waving and calling out her name. She runs towards him, screaming, "Dad, I'm coming to you!" but her voice has no sound. The faster she runs, the farther he seems to be. Still, she runs faster, harder. Clouds of white merciless mist block her from reaching him. "Dad, don't go!" she cries out in her head. But now, his image is fading, melting into the blanket of whiteness and silence.

Two years after her father's disappearance, her mother started dating a dentist from the Help Group. Short, bald with a terrible case of bad breath, the dentist was the complete opposite of her father. It wasn't long before *Dr. Halitosis* married her mom and moved into their home.

"Cristal, get off the computer. You have school tomorrow," her mother called out from the living room.

"Mom, fifteen more minutes!"

Fifteen minutes usually meant an hour.

"You know how your dad hates you playing those online games. He's going to be home soon."

"He's not my dad," she grumbled under her breath. *Why does Mom put up with that creep?*

Instead of hanging out at the malls like most thirteen-year-old girls, she spent her spare time battling against evil. It was about the time when she received a full scholarship to study at MIT, the summer before her fifteenth birthday, when she first met Harry.

She had gained ten million points, the most any player had ever reached. Everyone was talking about it in the discussion forums. That same day, she received a private message, which invited her to join the Elite team. It was sent by Harry, or more accurately by his online alias *Zero Doubt*, creator of the Truth Seekers. All gamers knew that *Zero* only invited the best of the best.

Zero: Inviting you to be a member of the Elite Team. You have twenty-four hours to accept the invitation.

No one would even dream of receiving a private message from the infamous *Zero Doubt*. When Harry posted a message, gamers would rush to reply to his post in hopes that he would respond. Unlike them, she wasn't a *fanboy*.

However, the challenge to be in the top team was hard to resist.

Mist: Mission accepted. Awaiting further instructions.

After the first successful mission as an elite Truth Seeker, Harry began messaging her regularly. They started to spend hours online brainstorming strategic maneuvers to conquer other players in the game.

Many times while video chatting with him, her stepfather would bang on her door yelling, "If you don't stop playing on the computer, I'm going to shut off the Internet!"

"Is everything okay?" Harry would ask her.

"Yeah," she answered.

Pretending things were fine kept her safe. "Never show anyone your weaknesses," her father always told her. "Especially your closest allies."

CHAPTER 5
SERENA (ALIAS LIONESS)

S erena leaned over and kissed her father on the cheek. He barely moved, his eyes glued to his iPad, reviewing his notes from his consular meetings that day.

"Good night, Father."

He mumbled something that resembled "Good night," kissed the top of her head, and returned to his notes. She straightened herself, turned, and walked out of the sitting room. Ever since the riot that devastated downtown Manila and the reports of hundreds of people who went missing a few weeks ago, her father had stayed past office hours at the consulate every night.

Her thoughts raced as she walked down the long dark corridor. Due to the blackouts in the city, everyone had to conserve electricity by keeping the lights off as much as possible. The huge three-story house was intimidating in the daytime but even spookier at nighttime.

Suddenly, Serena felt a hand on her left shoulder. Parts of her wanted to start running, but instead, she froze in her tracks. The spicy scent of "*Gucci pour Homme*" cologne enveloped her nostrils.

She must have sprayed that scent on thousands of male customers last summer at her part-time job during the "Shangri-la Plaza's Back to School" promotion. *Definitely, not a ghost.*

"Don't be scared, Serena. We need to talk," a deep, strong voice whispered in her ear.

This clown was about to learn he was messing with the wrong girl. All she needed was an opening and her training would kick in. She continued walking down the hall. The stranger pressed his hand into the small of her back.

She squinted to see her reflection in the twenty-foot mirror at the end of the hallway. Her short, dirty blonde hair pulled back in a ponytail, revealed her pale white skin. Her pink cotton pyjamas made her look like a bewildered child and not the confident twenty-two-year-old she was known to be among her circle of friends.

As they walked closer towards the mirror, she could faintly see the outline of her captor; his hooded jacket hid his facial features. Possibly six feet tall, his frame overshadowed her mere five-foot-two inches of height. She made mental notes, so if he got away after she disabled him, she'd have all the details to give to the police.

"Let's go inside your room."

It was more of a request than a command.

Why did he sound so familiar? Who was this person? She opened the door into the darkness of the room. Her hand reached out for the light switch, an automatic reaction. He grabbed her hand and held it tight.

"Keep the lights down for now."

The streaks of pale moonlight streamed through the open window onto her bed.

Serena tried to think. She could have easily caught her captor by surprise and kneed him in the groin or better yet, gouged his eyes out if she wanted to. Having taught self-defense classes at Global Nation for the past two years, she was not about to lose her advantage of her hidden talent until she ascertained what kind of weapon he carried.

"Have a seat on the bed."

Unsure of what his intentions were and yet as equally curious, she sat down on the corner of her bed, obeying his request. Her gaze moved up his dark pants and up his jacket until it reached his face. He raised his arm. She held her breath anticipating a blow, but realized he was only removing his hoodie from his head.

Before she could react, he sat down beside her and removed the backpack from his shoulder and lowered it onto the bed, keeping it close to him. He fumbled for a minute and brought out a square object. He placed it onto his lap and then opened it. The bright light from the laptop caught her by surprise and forced her to rule out robbery, rape, or kidnapping as a motive. He had to be the lamest intruder on the planet.

Unable to contain herself, she jumped up and said in a loud voice, "What is this? Who the hell are you?"

He turned to her, his blue eyes piercing into hers. His lips curled into a smile, like a child who had a secret to share.

"Harry...Harry Doubt. Nice to finally meet you in person, Serena, or should I say, *Lioness*? I have a mission for you. Many Philippine citizens have 'disappeared' or have gone missing in the last year."

"Are you nuts?" Serena sputtered. "You don't break into peoples' houses and say, 'Hi, I have a mission for you.' I want you to leave."

Serena stood, pointing at the door.

"Perhaps I went about this the wrong way," Harry said with a sigh.

"Ya' think?"

Harry reached out to shake her hand in an attempt to introduce himself. Serena grabbed it and made a swift classic *"ippon seoinage"* judo move, disabling Harry with a one-arm shoulder throw to the ground. She pinned her foot over his throat and twisted his arm. *That teaches you a lesson.*

"So talk to me. What's this about?" she asked.

"Manila, Global Nation," Harry managed to choke out. "Disappearances."

"So? Tell me something I don't know. Global Nation has been offering help to the local police and army to investigate the disappearances."

She pushed her foot even more firmly on his throat.

"In my front pocket of my shirt, there's a flash card. Take it."

She reached for the flash card while keeping an eye on him.

"We need you to find out what is on your father's computer. We have information that GN is involved."

CHAPTER 6
BEFORE ALL HELL BREAKS LOOSE

C ristal glanced at her watch. She had been standing outside the Global Nation's building for almost thirty minutes. *What was taking Kerim so long?*

She started to text him when she heard an engine roar from a distance. Kerim, aka *Shadow*, dressed in a leather jacket and black jeans was riding into the Global Nation's parking lot on his black and yellow Ducati.

He decelerated until he came up to the entrance, stopping in front of her. He removed his black helmet, his dark wavy hair slicked back against his head. When he took his sunglasses off, his grey steel eyes reflected the sunlight.

He waved for her to climb onto the back of the bike and handed her an extra helmet.

"No, hello?" she asked.

When he didn't reply, she took the helmet and put it over her head.

Kerim revved the engine.

"Let's get moving," he said. "Harry's video chat starts in 15 minutes."

Breathing in her own stale breaths and adjusting to the loss of peripheral view inside the full-face helmet was becoming more difficult than she'd imagined.

She climbed on the bike less smoothly than she would have preferred, grabbing onto Kerim's shoulder several times to keep from slipping.

"Hold tight, Cristal," he called back to her, revving the engine again.

She was intrigued by his accent, wondering where he was originally from.

"It's Turkish," said a voice in her head.

Weird.

She shut her eyes clenching her teeth, the vibration of the engine rumbling through her as he pulled out of the driveway. Kerim made a sharp turn, and she clutched onto him as they sped through the streets. She shut her eyes tighter, her heart pounding hard against her ribs, her head spinning inside the heaviness of the helmet.

Enclosed places seemed to trigger her so-called 'asthma attacks,' a term her father used to assure her mother she was normal. The breathing exercises he'd taught her to help stop oncoming attacks were difficult to do with a helmet strapped on her head.

The bike weaved in and out of traffic, honks and shouts from angry drivers filled her ears. The bike sped up weaved to the right and then stopped. She opened her eyes and sat back releasing her grip from Kerim's leather jacket. Tilting her head, she was relieved to see the familiar grey stone facade of Gabriel's apartment building.

Kerim climbed off the bike, removed his helmet and offered his hand. *He wasn't much of a talker.*

She tried to tell him that she didn't need any help but she swayed off balance, her legs betraying how dizzy and nauseous she felt.

She felt his arm around her waist, steadying her from keeling over. *Can't breathe! Need to get this helmet off.*

As if hearing her thoughts, Kerim reached over with his other hand, unsnapped the strap under her chin, and gently removed the helmet. The refreshing breeze brushed the dampness off her face. She welcomed the fresh air, inhaling deeply and exhaling slowly.

Shaky from the ride, she let herself relax against him, his arm still wrapped around her waist.

Up close she was able to see that his skin was a smooth olive color; his nose perfectly straight and Romanesque, and his grin mischievous but playful.

Once she regained her strength, she gently pulled away from his grasp. Yes, there was something appealing about him but outward appearances were only superficial assets. And yet, she always seemed to be drawn to the James Dean 'rebel without a cause' type. Just like her chocolate ice cream addiction, she had to stay away from bad boys, even if they were delicious desserts.

Focus on the mission.

She made her way to the entrance of the building and entered the buzzer number, leaving Kerim standing by his bike. The sound of the ring tone rang out several times until Gabriel's voice echoed out from the speaker.

"Yeah?"

"Gabriel, it's me, Cristal."

"C'mon in."

A loud "beep beep beep" sound came from the speaker. Kerim stepped in front, pulled the glass door, and held it open.

"Entrez-vous, Mademoiselle," he said with a small grin.

"Thanks." She walked past him into the lobby towards the elevators trying to avoid eye contact.

The building was built in the 1940s; the lighting was poor, the walls covered in fake orange suede flower wallpaper, probably from a previous renovation, and the carpet, once a bright red, was now a greyish brown. The outdated interior design wasn't what made her stomach queasy. What creeped her out was the strange feeling of someone (or something) watching her every time she was in the building.

Out of the corner of her eye, she could see Kerim watching her. She jabbed the button for the elevator and focused her eyes forward.

"Everything, ok?" he asked.

She gave a curt nod. "Of course."

The elevator arrived, creaking and squeaking as the doors opened. She stepped inside, pressed the button. Kerim walked to the the opposite side and leaned back, staring at her profile. She fidgeted with the strap on her backpack, an annoying self-conscious habit she thought she'd shaken.

Stop being distracted. Guys like him think they can melt a girl's heart with a little attention. You've been burned before.

Her thoughts brought flashbacks of Global Nation University during a tutoring session with her classmate Mikail who had out of the blue asked her out for dinner. Harry's response about her upcoming big date was to say Mikael was a dumb shmuck only out for one thing. The date ended up being a disaster just as he had predicted. Mikael *did* only want one thing.

After a breathtaking kiss, Mikael whispered in her ear, "Hey, can you work on my final term paper?"

Kerim chuckled to himself jolting Cristal back to the present.

She shot him a glare.

"What's so funny?"

He looked down at his boots, trying hard to stop.

"Nothing," he said.

The elevator lurched to a stop, the doors sliding open. Cristal stepped into the hall and began walking ahead. Even after all these years, she felt awkward and different. No matter how sophisticated she had become, she knew she was still a geek. Choice between a good book or a night out clubbing, she chose the good book. Hacking into secure networks was what she called entertainment.

She walked down the dark hallway in silence. The crackle of old incandescent bulbs hanging from the ceiling, accompanied the sound of their footsteps. His presence was comforting despite the initial irritation.

She stopped in front of Gabriel's apartment door and gave it a knock.

An unshaven Gabriel, his dreadlocks tied up in a short ponytail, poked his head out from behind the door. He gave her his usual goofy grin and was dressed in a worn grey bathrobe, T-shirt and jogging pants, his usual "all-night" gaming outfit.

Kerim coughed loudly before she could introduce him. Gabriel's eyes widened, his smile quickly disintegrating into a grim line.

"Who are you?" he demanded.

"Kerim Ilgaz," Kerim replied. "I was recruited to the Truth Seekers last week."

Gabriel narrowed his eyes, not so easily convinced. "Harry never mentioned you. And he never said you'd be coming."

Cristal was stumped. Harry was always careful about who he recruited and he never kept Gabriel, his most trusted Truth Seeker, in the dark.

Ever since he got her the job at Global Nation, Harry had been acting strange. Okay, stranger than usual. Who could blame him for being different? The guy had the IQ of Einstein for crying out loud. In her books, Harry's intense and introverted behavior was what made him intriguing. And sure, his idea of taking the Truth Seeker game offline seemed crazy at the time. When he said that the mission was to help her find her missing father, she was all in. After that, there was no looking back.

"Gabriel, we're here to find our parents. Come on, let us in," she said.

He gave her a glazed look. She stepped closer, letting her eyes meet his stare.

With an authoritative tone, she said, "You know I am the only

one who can decode all that encrypted data. Harry told me specifi-
cally to bring Kerim. Do you want to find your dad or not?"

Gabriel pressed his lips together for a moment before shrugging
his shoulders.

"Okay, whatever, come in," he said, stepping back.

Kerim walked past them, headed straight to the living room, and
plopped down on the black leather couch, placing his helmet beside
him. Cristal gave Gabriel a weak smile as she passed. She found a
spot at the opposite end of the couch, physically distancing herself
from Kerim.

"Hey, Gabe, do you have any coffee? I've got a terrible migraine,"
Kerim said.

Gabriel's brows shot up but met Cristal's gaze which pleaded
with him to play nice.

"Sure, I'll make a pot of Joe's," he said.

Gabriel disappeared into the kitchen, which was really part of
the living/dining room, separated only by a 1970s' style orange
beaded curtain. They used to tease him when he brought out his
round table and play his vinyl records of classic disco hits.

"Okay, so now what?" Kerim asked.

She brought out her laptop and placed it on the coffee table,
pushing the empty food wrappers and pizza boxes to the side.

The terminal was open on her screen. Kerim shifted closer to her,
his knee a fraction of an inch away from hers. She glanced down and
moved her knee away.

"Do you think you can really decode the encrypted file? Harry
seems to think so. But we all know that he has a crush on you." He
gave her a wry grin.

Focusing on the code, she let her fingers fly across the keyboard.
The characters and numbers flashed before her, comforting in its
simplicity. No emotional misunderstandings or tension to deal with
—just pure, straightforward code.

Gabriel came in balancing coffee mugs on a tray.

"Clear a space for me," he said. "This thing is getting heavy."

Kerim pushed the garbage off the coffee table and stood up.

"Let me help. Here give that to me," he said.

The tray wobbled and slipped from Gabriel's hands sending boiling coffee in all directions.

"Hey! Take it easy, man!" Kerim cried out.

"I handed it to you and you dropped it," Gabriel said, reaching out and grabbing the box of tissues from the table.

Kerim turned to Cristal, coffee dripping down from his pants to the carpet.

"He's a supreme klutz. Pass me the box of tissues, please," he said.

Gabriel's fists clenched. "Who are you calling a klutz?"

Kerim reached out and grabbed the box of tissues and began blotting his jeans. "I was referring to you but I guess that went over your head," he said.

Instead of getting the data for the video chat meeting with Harry, Cristal had to babysit the boys.

"You know, you're a real jerk," Gabriel growled.

"What did you say?" Kerim asked in a dangerously quiet voice.

"Oh, you heard what I said," Gabriel said, his eyes blazing.

He lunged towards Kerim, swinging at him. Kerim smoothly turned his body avoiding the punch. He grabbed Gabriel by the wrist and twisted his arm behind his back.

"You've got to be kidding me," Cristal said with a sigh.

Just then, her hands began to shake. *Oh, not again!* She needed to get out of there before anything happened. She grabbed her laptop and backpack.

"Where are you going?" Gabriel asked with his hand still locked behind his back.

"Yeah, where are you off to?" Kerim added, letting Gabriel's arm go.

She whirled around to face them.

"I don't know about you but I want to find my dad. Obviously you two only want to arm wrestle."

She walked past them towards Gabriel's bedroom. In the corner of the room were a twin-sized bed and a bookshelf full of action figure dolls. The bed was unmade; plastered on the wall were posters of video games and 70s music bands.

She put her laptop down on the desk and opened the video chat window.

Before she could continue with the decoding, she knew that she needed to calm down. The shaking episodes that used to overpower her in her teens only came about when she was extremely stressed. She used her deep breathing exercise to stop herself from shaking.

Stop thinking about it and it will go away.

She sank down on the chair and closed her eyes. She took in a deep breath and then let out a long exhale just as her father had taught her.

"*Be careful, Cristal,*" her father's voice hummed in her head.

After a few minutes of deep breathing, the shaking stopped.

"Are you okay?"

She opened her eyes and saw Gabriel and Kerim standing in the doorway looking like repentant little boys begging forgiveness from their mother.

"Yeah, I'm fine," she replied. "Did you guys make peace?"

Gabriel lips curled into a smile.

He turned to Kerim and said, "Hey, how did you learn those cool self-defense moves?"

"I was in the Turkish Army for four years for mandatory service," Kerim said.

"Could you teach me some of that? I'm really good at fighting in the game, but man, it would be really cool to be able to do it for real."

Gabriel threw him a fake punch to his stomach.

Kerim doubled over. They began fake wrestling together, bumping into the doorframe.

"Okay, boys. Are you guys done yet?" Cristal said, relieved that they were no longer at each other's throats.

Suddenly, a high-pitched sound blasted into the room knocking the action figures off the shelf. The floor began shaking beneath her feet. She paused for a moment, wondering if she was causing this. She looked at her hands. They were steady and she noticed too that her breathing was even. *But I stopped shaking. This shouldn't be happening.*

She glanced up to see Gabriel's hand on the doorframe and the other one holding onto Kerim's chest, his eyes closed tight. Kerim's arms were outstretched, his hands holding onto the doorframe. His eyes were staring at her, wide open; his face pale.

Her multiple experiences with the room shaking, minus the high-pitched sound, made her relatively calm despite what was happening. As if in a dream, she watched in slow motion her laptop slide off the desk along with her mouse, the jar of pens and other miscellaneous office supplies.

HER CHAIR SEEMED to sway with the waves of turbulence, almost as if the legs had shock absorbers attached. Although the shaking seemed to be in slow motion for her, she knew that it wasn't the same for Kerim and Gabriel. She could see the doorframe shaking violently, the wall almost seeming like it was going to implode. For brief instances, it seemed that Kerim and Gabriel disappeared into thin air. *Freak, I'm seeing things now.*

She opened her mouth to call out to them but the thunderous roar around them muted her voice. It seemed like hours but really was only seconds later when the floor stopped shaking. She noticed that the high-pitched sound had also vanished. Everything grew eerily still.

Kerim let go of the doorframe with Gabriel still clutching to him with his eyes closed.

"Oh!" Gabriel whimpered.

After a few seconds, he opened one eye and looked around, then glancing up to see Kerim's raised brow. He stepped away.

"I mean, wow that was really amazing, huh?" Gabriel said.

Kerim pushed Gabriel aside and rushed towards Cristal.

"Are you okay?" he asked.

She gave him a thumbs up yet still unsure if she were the cause of what seemed to be a mini earthquake.

"Yeah, I'm okay."

What just happened here? Was it an earthquake or was the shaking isolated to the room? So many thoughts were filling her mind.

Kerim bent down to pick up her laptop. The light from the screen was still on—a good sign that all her work was not lost.

"Looks like your laptop is just as tough as you," Kerim said, while placing the computer back on top of the desk.

On the screen, the video chat window was open, and Harry and Joanna were watching them.

Joanna's mouth was wide open, her eyes wide with shock. Harry was grinning from ear to ear. He was speaking, but there was no sound. Behind them, people were picking up things off the ground. From what Cristal could make of it, they were mostly cups, cutlery, and overturned chairs.

Cristal reached over and pressed the volume button until Harry's voice was audible. Gabriel came over and stood behind her while Kerim moved to the other side.

"...that was spectacular, guys. Dr. Saeed and I were working on some tests. We believe we are closer to proving my father's theory. We want to talk to all of you in person tonight. I will text you the details."

CHAPTER 7
QUESTIONS THAT NEED ANSWERS

CRISTAL STARED AT HER monitor in disbelief. The video chat window went black.

"Were you in on this?" Gabriel asked, turning to her.

Cristal said, "No," and sat back.

Suddenly Kerim leaned towards her, grabbed the chair's armrests with both hands and spun her chair towards him. With his hands still on the armrests, he leaned over and looked directly into her eyes.

She heard Gabriel ask, "What was that, guys?"

Kerim's eyes seemed to be shooting accusations into hers while she was trying to process what Harry had told them.

"You were very calm during the whole thing," he said to her raising one eyebrow.

She stared back, not one to be easily intimidated. She could hear Gabriel moving around behind her.

"She didn't seem calm to me," Gabriel said.

Kerim tilted his head towards him.

"Gabriel, you had your eyes closed the whole time."

She felt her body relax for a moment.

"Well, not the whole time," Gabriel replied. "Okay, most of it."

Kerim's eyes met hers causing her body to tense up again.

"Before you answer, Cristal," Kerim said, "I want to know, can we trust him?"

He pointed at Gabriel.

"Hey! Wait a minute!" Gabriel cried out.

She shoved her chair back, releasing Kerim's death grip on the chair, forcing him to stand up. She looked from Gabriel to Kerim. *Question is, can I trust either of them?*

"If you really want to know..." she said.

Gabriel pleaded with his eyes for her to continue.

"This isn't the first time this happened to me."

Gabriel leaned back on the desk, his mouth open in astonishment.

"What do you mean?"

Kerim knelt beside her, placing his hands on the arm rests, his steel grey eyes searching hers, digging into her mind for answers.

"Do you want to know what I saw, Cristal?" Kerim asked in a low voice.

Her body felt paralyzed.

Kerim continued, "*You* started the earthquake and the bright light, right?" he asked in a hypnotic tone.

Cristal clenched her fists and stood up. She leaned in towards him, planting her fists on her hips.

"Is this an interrogation, Kerim?" she asked.

She sensed her emotions getting out of control.

"I was watching you and there was a beam of light coming out from your chest to the ceiling and it bounced back to the ground. It was like the light was coming through you."

Kerim took a step forward, approaching her with caution.

Her hands fell to her side. Despite wanting to leave, she forced herself to listen.

"I don't know anything about that," she said.

"When the room was shaking, you were motionless. Your eyes were empty. But I could see things above your head."

Gabriel threw him a look.

"What things?"

"I don't know how to explain it," Kerim continued. "It was like watching a movie from an old projector onto the white screen. Except the screen was the light that was coming out from inside you."

She blinked in astonishment. *That's impossible. I have to get out of here.*

"Cristal, did you feel or see any of that?" Gabriel asked. "Are you okay?"

"No, I'm not okay. I don't have to stay here and listen to this."

She leaped up, bumping Gabriel aside as she grabbed her laptop and backpack and headed to the door.

Kerim and Gabriel tailed her. Before she opened the door, she felt Kerim's hand on her shoulder.

"Cristal, you can't leave now. We need to talk about this," Kerim said.

Who the heck does he think he is?

"No, we don't. I need to go and find Harry. Let me go."

She pushed his hand away.

"Harry?" Gabriel asked.

She noted the sound of concern in his voice.

"No, I agree with Kerim. We need to figure this out as much as we can before meeting Harry and the rest of the group tonight."

She couldn't think properly much less talk about it. *Beam of light? Projections above my head? What next?*

Just then, her cell phone beeped. She scrambled to get it out of her backpack. New text message from Harry. The sound of Gabriel and Kerim's cell phone text message ringtones followed soon after.

Zero: Meet me at the GN University, Physics Dept., Room 1130 at 6 pm today. Confirm receipt.

She started to type a text back when her phone started ringing. Harry's name came up on the screen. She swiped the screen to answer.

"Yes?" Cristal asked.

"Checking to see if you're okay."

Harry's voice seemed serious, but she could hear a hint of excitement. His phone call should have calmed her, but she was feeling more anxious than ever.

"No, not really. What were you talking about earlier? What tests?" she said.

Should I tell Harry about the light that Kerim saw? No. Don't tell him anything until I figure out what he is up to.

"I'll meet you back at GN and we can talk then," he said.

Before she could say anything, he ended the call.

CHAPTER 8
WHO TO TRUST

CRISTAL'S THOUGHTS WERE rattling in her head like a pinball machine, each one banging into the other.

"I have to go," she said still staring at her phone.

"Okay, I'll drop you off," Kerim replied.

He went into the living room grabbing his helmet off the couch.

"No, I'm taking a cab back to the office."

Kerim appeared startled by her response.

"Okay, then. See you tonight," Kerim said slowly.

Gabriel stared at her with a look of concern.

"We should talk about this some more, but that's just what I think," he mumbled to himself.

Maybe Gabriel is right. She paused for a moment but then shook her doubts from her head and walked out the door.

OUTSIDE THE BUILDING, she welcomed the fresh air. She stood still for a moment, taking in deep breaths, hoping to relax. She looked around. People were scattering on the streets like the fire ants that used to seek safety from the garden hose she used to wield on in the backyard of her childhood home.

"There is no signal," a young man said to her. He was waving his cell phone. "Do you have a signal?"

She shook her head, knowing full well that her cell phone was working fine. It was connected to a satellite and not on a regular cellular network. Harry had made sure that all the Truth Seekers were able to communicate with each other at all times.

She glanced down at her phone and noticed there was a text message from Serena.

Lioness: We just had a small earthquake here in Manila. No physical damage but lots of people are saying they saw weird things. Like visions... Will send you pics soon.

WHAT? An earthquake in the Philippines too? She began typing a response when she noticed some commotion on the corner of the intersection.

A group of teenagers on the corner were pointing towards the sky. She tilted her head to see what the big deal was. Something was very different. Angry strokes of crimson red with charcoal rain clouds hung above them. Streaks of lightning were crisscrossing each other like an intricate woven rug. If she squinted, she could make out an image, almost like a painting. The image of a middle aged woman was becoming more vivid and clear.

I must be seeing things. Have to get out of here.

She scurried down West 34th Street praying to find a cab that could take her out of the chaos but abandoned cars were making the normally traffic congested street even more difficult for cabs to get through. She started picking up her pace, half walking, half running.

She had to get to GN, which was on Lexington and East 33rd Avenue, probably a good twenty-five-minute walk.

Pockets of people passed her by, their eyes opened wide, blinking fast as she raced past them. A woman with snow-white hair and clear blue eyes caught her gaze. She was walking towards her, clutching her black purse, her shoes with thick black heels hitting the ground making a sound like a crack of thunder with each step. Cristal covered her ears hoping to block the sound. *Walk past her. Look away.*

She tried to avoid making eye contact, but her eyes were drawn back to the woman. The old lady was now stopped in front of her raising her crooked finger at her.

"It was you. You were in my vision during the earthquake."

Cristal froze, the old lady's words crawling into her skull. Her skin felt like fire ants crawling up her arms.

"I don't know what you mean," she said, half believing her own words.

The woman continued, clutching the gold cross around her neck like it was the only thing keeping her alive. "It was you. There was a bright light coming down from heaven through your body into the earth."

Cristal shook her head and said firmly, "No, not me! It wasn't me."

She yanked her arm away from the old woman and started sprinting down the street. Her heart was pounding; her palms sweating as she ran. Her backpack bounced against her and the straps rubbed against her shoulders.

She kept running, oblivious of the people bumping into her. The words repeated in her head like a mantra.

"It wasn't me. It wasn't me!"

She looked up and realized that GN was at the next corner. Dodging traffic, she jaywalked across the street. As she ran up to the busy intersection, another voice entered her head.

"But it was you, darling."

CHAPTER 9
EARTHQUAKE OR NOT?

CRISTAL'S PULSE WAS RACING, her lungs gasping for air. *"Was it me?"* she asked herself.

She felt as though she had just finished doing the 100-mile sprint of her life. Imagine being frightened of a little defenceless granny. Deep down inside, the fear was like lead weighing down her gut. She had to get to Harry to get some answers.

She pushed her way past the people on the street and ran across the intersection. Some GN staff were standing in clusters all around the designated safe areas. She saw members from her team gathering at the end of the street. She weaved her way through the crowd, searching for Harry. She could hear comments as she walked past.

"It's the climate change that did this," a lady from the accounting department said.

"I bet you it had something to do with terrorists," another said.

"It was scary. I thought we were going to die," a man from the Helpdesk support team told a fellow team member.

As she came closer, the sound of their voices filled her head. The sound was rising as if someone had cranked up the volume full blast. She needed to calm down and take control of herself.

Get out of my head! She closed her eyes and slowed her breathing.

It was working. The voices were fading, except for one. Harry's.

"Cristal, is everything okay?"

She opened her eyes to find Harry staring at her intensely. A wave of relief swept through her body until she noticed Joanna beside him, clutching onto Harry's arm as if she were holding onto him for dear life.

Cristal wanted answers but not to the expense of having Joanna listening in.

"Harry, we need to talk."

Harry must have noticed Cristal's anxiety. He glanced down and pulled his arm from Joanna's vice-like grip. Joanna put on a show by glaring at him, crossing her arms and pouting.

"They're doing a head count," he said, switching back to Cristal.

"Good to know," Cristal replied.

"Can you take me home?" Joanna asked, tugging at Harry's arm. Harry shook his arm free, the expression on his face reflecting his irritation.

"Are you listening to me?" she whined.

He responded but his gaze never left Cristal's face.

"Joanna, calm down. After they give us the *all-clear* signal, we have to go back in."

"You're the manager! You can let us go home, if you wanted to," she said.

Cristal gritted her teeth. Patience with Joanna was not her strongest quality.

"Get a hold of yourself, Joanna," she said. "Be happy you're okay and stop being such a whiner."

"Okay? I'm NOT okay," Joanna blurted out. She waved her arms to emphasize her point. "None of this is okay!"

"Do you realize what happened today?" Cristal asked, her anger rising.

"No, duh. We had an earthquake," Joanna replied, rolling her eyes. "Right, Harry?"

Joanna turned to him with her hands on her hips.

"Tell us. Was that an earthquake?"

Harry gave her a dirty look.

"This is not the time or the place," he said quietly.

Out of the corner of Cristal's eye she sensed a presence standing beside her. She glanced up to see Kerim. *How did he get here so fast with the traffic jam?*

"Alleys, side streets and sidewalks," Kerim said.

It made her queasy Kerim knew exactly what she had been thinking.

The sound of a horn blast coming from the building filled the air, indicating that it was safe to enter the building. Kerim and Harry were standing toe to toe.

"Yeah, Harry, tell us if that was an earthquake," Kerim said.

"This is not the time nor the place," Harry repeated, narrowing his eyes.

He motioned to Cristal to go with him towards the building.

"See you at six tonight, Kerim," he said.

Cristal would've followed Harry. Technically he was her manager at GN although, her working there was only a cover to hack into the GN networks. But then again, Harry was the leader of the Truth Seekers and normally she never questioned his commands when it came to fulfilling their mission. Debating with herself, she found herself with a dilemma. *Do I go with Harry and spend the next few hours acting as if nothing happened?*

"We've got plans," she said.

She tucked her arm in Kerim's and pulled herself closer to him, causing Harry's eyebrows to shoot up.

She could feel Kerim's stare but he played along, placing his hand on hers. Anyone watching would think they were a couple.

"See you tonight," she said to Harry. "Kerim, let's go."

She smirked imagining the steam spewing from Harry's nostrils.

Joanna must have been enjoying the show because her smile was stretching wider with a glint of glee in her eyes.

Cristal thought, *I'm not as predictable as you think, Mr. Doubt.*

"Your ride awaits you, my lady," Kerim said, giving Harry a friendly wink, enjoying Cristal's tactical maneuver.

Cristal smiled to herself, letting him guide her away. She glanced back and caught Harry watching them. *What thoughts were running through his mind right now?*

She pulled Kerim's arm, urging him to pick up the pace.

"What's the hurry?" he asked.

"No hurry," she said. "I want to get away from this crowd."

He squeezed her hand reassuringly. They walked hand in hand until they reached the intersection. She turned back to see GN staff walking into the building.

So what next, she asked herself, realizing that she hadn't thought it through.

"My bike is over there in front of the coffee shop," Kerim said, interrupting her thoughts. "You want me to take you home? We've got a few hours to kill before the meeting tonight."

She realized that her hand felt good in his. *Why not play this out a bit?*

"Nah, I don't want you to have to drive through the chaos out there. I can take a cab after the meeting, assuming the streets will be clear by then. Let's go to the coffee shop instead. It should be open," she said.

"A good espresso might help my caffeine headache."

She glanced up at him and remarked, "You still have a headache?"

"Well I didn't get a chance to get my dose of caffeine at Gabriel's. And spilling it on my jeans doesn't count."

She giggled, remembering the event that happened earlier.

They crossed the street in silence and stopped in front of

the shop.

"I guess Harry can't see us anymore," he said quietly.

He gently let go of her hand.

"Yes, sorry for that," she said. "Thanks for helping me back there. I really didn't want to hang out with Harry right now."

He stared at her for a moment. His steely gazes made her catch her breath. She remembered her thoughts from earlier about ice cream and bad boys. *Chocolate ice cream is very bad for your hips*, she reminded herself.

"No worries. I know how it is," he said, snapping her back to reality.

She gave him a small smile realizing that her cheeks were probably the color of persimmon.

Cristal wished she could enjoy this moment with Kerim a little longer but they reached the coffee shop's entrance. The sign on the door said "Open" so despite the earthquake, it looked like the shop was running business as usual.

"After you," Kerim said, pulling open the door.

Inside the owner of the shop was sweeping the floor behind the counter. He looked up when he noticed them standing in the entrance.

"Sorry, we're closed."

She started to turn around, but Kerim's hand gently squeezed her arm.

"We were hoping we could stay here for a bit. We really have nowhere to go right now," he said.

The man behind the counter stopped sweeping and stared intently at them as Kerim continued with his story.

"She's not feeling well. Something fell on her head during the earthquake. We just need a few moments."

She touched her head, wincing slightly and hoped that it looked convincing.

The shop owner leaned the broom against the back wall and

walked towards them, wiping his hands on his apron.

"It's been a hell of a day," he said. "Please come and sit at this table."

He pulled back a chair and waited for Cristal to sit down.

"Do you want anything? Tea, coffee? An ice pack?"

As she sat down, she smiled and said, "I'm fine. Thanks for asking. I just need to rest a moment."

"I'll have an espresso," Kerim added, winking at her as he sat down across the small table. "And how about an iced café for the lady?"

"Of course, no problem," the owner said, and then walked back to the counter.

Cristal leaned towards Kerim and whispered, "You like starting trouble, don't you?"

"I was just trying to be a gentleman. Besides, I need my caffeine fix."

Maybe now they could have a real conversation together. Who knew that this would be the sweet "aftershock" following the stunt she pulled on Harry earlier?

"I guess I could do with an iced café after all we've been through."

He leaned forward, and admitted in a semi-sultry voice, "Now I've revealed my weakness to you."

"You're hilarious," she said, putting her hands on the table. "My dad always said, 'Never reveal your weaknesses.'"

"You have a very wise father," he said.

His steel grey eyes probed hers, looking for what... she wasn't sure. The sadness that she buried deep down inside suddenly welled up in her throat.

"Yes, he is..." she half-whispered, "or was."

She looked down at the table.

"I'm sorry. I didn't mean to..." Kerim reached for her hand.

She tried to blink away the tears that betrayed the cold loneliness she felt all the time. A loneliness that had become part of her since the day her father disappeared.

"He went missing when I was a kid."

Cristal focused her eyes on Kerim, telling herself to calm down. The only time she had ever shared personal information about her father was with Harry.

"But I know he'll be back."

"I understand. My older brother went MIA when I was in the Army," he said.

Cristal noticed his other hand clenched into a fist.

"Missing in action?"

"Yes," he said in a quiet voice, and then he turned his head to look out the window.

She put her other hand on top of his.

He cleared his throat, and said, "Okay, let's talk about what happened today."

He gently pulled his hand away from hers.

"Yes, let's do that."

She leaned back.

"I don't think there was an earthquake," he said quietly. "I know you feel the same way."

Her pulse began racing.

The shop owner walked towards them with their drinks.

"Thank you very much," she said, relieved by the distraction.

"Do you mind turning on the TV?" Kerim asked him.

"Sure, I didn't even bother checking if the cable was working."

He went to the counter, grabbed the remote, pointed it towards the large flat screen TV, and turned it on. The local news station came up on the screen and the anchorwoman was speaking, but there was no sound. He pressed the button to turn up the volume.

"...reports from Manila, Rome, Gaza, Haifa, and Vancouver confirm that earthquakes occurred at the precise time as the one that hit Manhattan at 1:25 p.m. Eastern Standard Time today."

CHAPTER 10
WANT SOME ANSWERS

I T WAS SEVEN HOURS AFTER the earthquake. Dr. Saeed, dressed in his white lab coat, over black casual slacks and a Ford dress shirt, and wearing his Boss glasses on top of his head, stood at the front of the classroom alongside Harry. His hair was combed back and his face was clean-shaven.

His real name was Dr. Saeed Nariman but students had such a hard time pronouncing his last name, so he asked everyone to call him Dr. Saeed instead. Out of all the professors, Cristal always thought Dr. Saeed was the most stylish prof at the university. Three video chat windows were opened on the projection screen. Cristal was sitting on a stool in the first row of lab tables. Gabriel sat beside her with Kerim on the other side. Joanna sat front and center of the tables, positioned in clear view of Harry, purposely blocking Cristal's view.

Cristal entertained the thought of reaching over and smacking the back of her head. Kerim's knee hit hers.

She turned to him and mouthed the words *"What?"*

He tossed her a half grin.

Is he reading my mind? She shivered at the thought, and then focused her attention on the screen.

Serena was speaking. Her dirty blonde hair was swept up with a clip. From what Cristal could tell, Serena was in what looked like her bedroom.

"I was at the location as requested for my mission. The news reports have confirmed that it was the precise epicenter of the earthquake. I also confirmed that there were no early warnings as reported on the HEWS Seismic webpage. For those of you who are not familiar, HEWS is the Humanitarian Early Warning System."

Serena glanced down at her notes.

"I have further confirmation from seismologists around the world that no one expected these earthquakes."

In the other video chat window, the Martinelli twins, Rinaldo and Angelica, codenames *Red Fox* and *Venus*, were agreeing.

Cristal was eager to hear what Rinaldo had to say. It was hard to resist liking him. His wavy brown hair, hazel brown eyes and Hollywood smile, not to mention his quaint Italian accent, made the other Truth Seekers, mainly those of the female persuasion, rush to his assistance when he needed help in the game. In real life, at only five-foot-nine, he had no trouble attracting high-fashion models who towered over him.

"Yeah, it was pretty crazy here in Roma," he said, "Angelica and me were freakin' out over here when the earth-a-quake hit us. You can imagine that. I'm-a-sure that the Pope fell off his throne and I'm not-a talkin' about the one in the Vatican."

He flashed his contagiously charming smile. Angelica gave him a dirty look in return. Cristal had to hold back a giggle.

"Yes, I have to agree," Angelica said, turning to the camera. "It was a freaky experience. I cannot wait to-a-hear what *Zero* has to say about this. Please explain why and how you knew where we were supposed to be when it happened."

Angelica flipped her long wavy brown hair away from her dark mocha eyes. Cristal envied how Angelica could look both upset and sexy at the same time. Her naturally thick pouty lips were what women would pay thousands for in Botox treatments. Cristal looked over at Kerim, trying to read his body language as he listened.

Kerim's face was expressionless. He was listening but not reacting the way men usually do when they see Angelica for the first time. Gabriel, who was sitting on the other side of Cristal, was gazing at the screen. She could have sworn he was drooling as he smiled, drinking in Angelica's every word.

Cristal looked back at the screen and caught Harry's gaze. He was watching her closely. She took a deep breath and focused on what Angelica was saying.

"The room we were in was shaking so much. The floor beneath us, I swear, became like a jelly. Rinaldo and me were so frightened. He was holding onto me and crying like a bambina."

Everyone in the room laughed. Rinaldo raised his hand and smacked her on the shoulder.

"Ayyyy...what's a matter with you?" Angelica cried out, turning to him. "It's the truth. You were crying like a little baby girl."

She playfully hit him on the back of his head.

"Let's-a-be serious," Rinaldo said, turning back towards them. "*Zero*, we want to know what in the world is going on."

He pointed his finger towards the camera.

Harry smiled and said, "Let's let our rep from Haifa report first. Adel, please tell us what happened at the two locations I asked you and your team to meet."

In the third window on the screen, a man that Cristal did not recognize began to speak. He had dark black hair, cut short on the sides, longer and wavy at the top. His eyebrows were thick over large eyes that sank deep into his head. He had a wide bridge over a broad nose and his skin was a cinnamon color.

"Hi, everyone. Nice to meet you. At the Gaza location, our team member, Sami, experienced the ground shaking. He was outside and

he saw in the sky, the light streaks, which he first reported as lightning. Then the sky turned blood red. He saw an image forming in
the sky like an oil painting. He sent us this picture."

A photo appeared on the screen. Harry moved the mouse and
maximized the image. In the picture, the sky was as Adel had
described. The sky appeared to be a burgundy red.

Cristal squinted and could see an image where the lightning
streaks were crossing each other.

Gabriel was shifting his weight on the stool beside her.

He whispered, "It looks like a man."

Cristal focused her eyes at the image again. It did look like a
man. As Harry zoomed into the area, the shape was becoming
clearer. It seemed as if the man was pointing in a direction to the
east of him. As the picture sharpened, Cristal could see the man's
facial features.

She gasped.

"Cristal, are you okay?" Kerim whispered in her ear.

She could feel herself fading out. The room seemed to be spinning around her. This is how Dorothy must have felt when her house
was being swept away by the tornado, she thought to herself.

She felt Kerim's arms around her as she slipped off her stool.

"Someone get her a glass of water! Cristal, are you okay?"

She felt herself being lowered to the floor. She closed her eyes, as
the thoughts in her head bounced back and forth like a shuffleboard
disc she had seen her stepfather play years ago on the deck of a
Disney cruise ship. He had proposed to her mother that same night,
much to her disgust.

"Cristal, this is Dr. Saeed."

She felt something cold pressed onto her forehead.

"We are just going to move you over to the couch, okay?"

She felt her body being lifted. *So this is what floating feels like.* Her
body was lowered onto the couch, her head gently placed onto something soft.

"Cristal, is it something you saw?" Harry asked.

"Leave her alone," she could hear Kerim snap. "Can't you see she needs to rest?"

"Is she okay?" Gabriel asked.

"She's just faking it," Joanna said.

If she could have lifted herself up, Cristal would have gone over and slapped the witch in the face. But her arms felt like concrete blocks; her legs were stiff and she was unable to move them.

"Can you try to take a sip of water?" Dr. Saeed asked softly in her ear.

She felt someone lift her upright. Her body leaned back against someone as she took a deep breath. *Kerim?* His cologne enveloped her nostrils. She started gasping and her eyelids snapped open.

"She's awake!" Gabriel cried out.

She looked up and saw Kerim on his knees. He was holding a small vial under her nose. The fumes overwhelmed her senses.

She raised her arm and pushed it away from her face.

"What is that?" she managed to say.

"Mr. Biker over here thought he could wake you up with his emergency backup bottle of cologne," Joanna answered.

Gabriel knelt down beside Kerim. He looked up towards Joanna who was standing behind them.

"It worked, didn't it?" Gabriel said.

He turned to Cristal.

"Kerim said that back in Istanbul, they always use cologne to revive people who faint."

She took a deep breath. Her head was becoming clear again. She struggled to sit up by herself. She noticed that it was Harry whom she had been leaning against. He was staring at her, and his gaze was filled with deep concern.

"Are you okay now?" he asked.

"I'm better," she replied, "but the room is still slightly spinning."

She put her arm out and grabbed Kerim's shoulder to steady herself. He reached out and held her.

She stood up, feeling lightheaded. Then she swooned, feeling her legs get weak. Harry, Kerim, and Gabriel jumped up. Each one of them held onto her to keep her from falling forward. Harry eased her back onto the couch.

"You need to rest," Dr. Saeed said, as he kneeled down in front of her.

He flashed a light into her eyes.

"Your eyes are dilated. You need to lie down and put your feet up."

He helped her lie down while Kerim put a pillow under her feet.

"Everyone, give her some space. She needs air," Kerim said.

Her eyelids felt like weights were forcing them shut.

"Come on, everyone. The meeting is over," he added.

She could hear people moving away.

"Dr. Saeed, I need to talk to her," Harry whispered, a few feet away from her.

"Kerim is right. She needs to rest. We can talk to her when she is better," Dr. Saeed replied.

"I'll stay with her. When she's stronger, I'll take her home," Kerim said.

Was he beside her?

"I think I should stay with her and you should go," Harry responded.

She heard shuffling and more whispering. Using what little energy she had left, she managed to speak.

"Kerim, don't go."

"She's delusional," she heard Harry say.

"You heard her," Kerim said. "I'll take her home. No need for both of you to stay here."

"Harry, why don't we move the meeting to my office? We can check on her in an hour or so," Dr. Saeed said.

She heard more shuffling, and then there was silence.

She was in a white room. Around her there were walls made out of clouds. She noticed that in her hand was a paintbrush covered in red paint. She turned around and one wall was covered in red with streaks of white clouds in between each stroke. The clouds started to move, bending the lines, and forming a picture. She put the paintbrush down and moved towards it. Each step she took was as if she were floating. Weightless. Free.

"*Cristal,*" a voice said.

Her eyes widened. The picture was coming to life.

"*Don't be afraid.*"

It was changing shape and moving towards her.

"Dad?"

CHAPTER 11
WHAT IS THIS ALL ABOUT?

CRISTAL EYES SNAPPED OPEN and darkness surrounded her. The dream was still clear in her mind. *But was it a dream?* She sat up, looked around, and saw that she was alone. *How long have I been sleeping? Where is everyone?*

She stood up, adjusting her eyes to the darkness and walked towards the doorway, bumping into a stool. She picked up her backpack, which was still sitting on the table. She walked out of the classroom into the dark hallway. She reasoned that the building was running on power from the generator, due to the earthquake. It was creepy being alone in the dark.

She could see light coming from Dr. Saeed's office across from the classroom. As she walked closer to the doorway, there were voices involved in an intense conversation. Slowly, she approached the door. Kerim was standing in front of Harry and Dr. Saeed in front of a desk, and they were seated at the meeting table. There was no one else in the room.

"...and that's what you really think happened? Time travel? C'mon Harry, I know there are strange things happening, but that?"

Harry was smiling, and his hands were animated as he spoke.

"Like I said earlier, it's all in my father's notes. Dr. Saeed was helping my father prove their theory that there are portals or black holes in locations around the world. My dad worked with Dr. Saeed to gather data from multiple sources that included satellite imagery, and a geographic information system."

He turned to Dr. Saeed. "Tell him about the experiments with the kids."

Dr. Saeed crossed his arms. "Aaron Doub theorized that gifted children's extra sensory skills could help connect or bridge the present to the future."

Harry's grin grew wider, as he said, "Child prodigies have natural abilities that are remarkable for children their age. My father believed that the reason for this is because their brains are able to process data and information like computers. His tests proved that they use fifty times more brain cells than average children or adults. They theorized that if we placed a gifted person at a location where a black hole or portal exists, it would be the key to unleash the energy to open up the portals."

The expression on Kerim's face said loud and clear that he wasn't buying anything they were saying to him. He sat down on the edge of the desk.

"So is that how the earthquakes happened?" Kerim inquired. "Gabriel's apartment is one of the locations of a black hole?"

Kerim leaned towards Harry and pointed his finger at him.

"That's why you wanted Cristal to go there. And you needed me to keep her safe. Is that it?" He paused. "When the earthquake happened, I saw a white light coming out of Cristal's chest that shot up to the ceiling and it went right through to the ground."

Cristal's heart started beating faster. *I can't believe Harry set me up.* She clenched her fists and felt her face turn red. She stepped closer to the door but kept herself from entering.

Kerim now had Harry and Dr. Saeed's full attention.

"What do you mean a white light?" Dr. Saeed asked, crossing his arms and tilting his head.

"Can you describe what it looked like?" Harry interrupted.

Kerim took a deep breath. "The light came from the ceiling down into her chest and then it went into the ground. I saw images above her head like a movie playing on a screen."

He paused, as if trying to recollect what he had seen.

"Go on," Harry said.

"Well, I saw you, Cristal, Dr. Saeed, Gabriel, Rinaldo, and Adel. I was there, too. There was another guy, dark-skinned, brown hair. I couldn't see him very well."

Dr. Saeed glanced at Harry and then looked back at Kerim. "Could be Sami?"

Kerim continued, "We were standing outside somewhere, and it was hot. The sun was hitting the grey wall behind us. Cristal moved to the center, and all of a sudden there was a white light coming out from her chest. It was weird, because it looked almost like a mirror of what was happening in front of me."

He sat back down on the edge of the desk and fell silent.

"Don't stop now," Harry said.

Kerim looked at Harry. His eyes narrowed as he spoke. "Harry, it was all about you, all this time! Right?"

Harry arched his eyebrow and stole a glance at Dr. Saeed, who was intently listening to Kerim.

"I don't know what you're talking about," Harry said.

Cristal heard the sincerity in his voice.

"You and Dr. Saeed over here are in on this, right?" Kerim demanded, pounding his fist onto the table.

Dr. Saeed showed no facial expressions. "Kerim, tell us what you saw," he said calmly.

Kerim stood up and turned towards Harry, his grey eyes piercing into his.

"You walked into the light," he said in a low voice.

Cristal had to step closer to hear him.

"Then the light disappeared."

Harry's eyebrows arched up. "And that's it?" he asked.

Kerim replied, "No, that isn't it."

Harry stood up, his gaze never leaving Kerim's. "Okay, so tell us."

"It wasn't just the light that disappeared. **You** disappeared with it."

Harry had a shocked look on his face, and his eyebrows were arching even higher. Dr. Saeed's eyes widened slightly. He leaned over and whispered something into Harry's ear. Harry smirked in agreement.

Kerim had turned around, seemingly oblivious to what was around him. He ran his hands through his hair in exasperation.

"And that's when the earthquake stopped. The light and the images vanished," he said.

A smile crept onto Harry's face. "In your vision, I must have traveled into the future!"

Cristal could feel her face burn red. She could not contain her fury any longer. She marched into the room. Everyone turned to look at her with stunned looks on their faces.

"That explains a lot, Harry," she said, her voice shaking with anger.

Cristal looked straight into his eyes. "But guess what? This prodigy wants nothing to do with your time traveling theory."

She whirled around, poking her finger onto Kerim's shoulder. "And you," she said, her voice rising higher.

She looked at her hands briefly realizing that they were beginning to shake. "I was beginning to trust you. Now I know better. I can't believe you told them about the light."

She turned around with full intentions of running out the door, but she stopped. On the shelf, among stacks of books was an 8x10 photo in a silver frame. In the photo, Dr. Saeed was standing on the far right. She recognized the man in the middle as Harry's father. She had seen his YouTube videos on the Truth Seekers' discussion forums. But it wasn't Aaron Doub that caught her eye. It was the woman on the other side of him.

She stepped closer, wondering where she had seen this person that appeared in the picture. Harry and Kerim walked up and stood beside her.

"That's her," Cristal managed to say, pointing to the picture.

"Who?" Kerim asked.

"After the earthquake, I looked up into the sky and saw a face. It was her." She could feel her heart pounding harder and faster.

"Are you sure?" Dr. Saeed asked.

"I'm positive," she answered. Her words seemed to stick in her throat like chalk dust.

Harry grabbed her by the shoulders and turned her towards him. His blue eyes were wide with excitement.

"That's Bina Schwartz. My mother."

"Are you serious?" Kerim asked.

"Yes!" he said. "She went missing last year."

CHAPTER 12
KISMET

S HE COULDN'T STOP RUNNING. Minutes earlier, she had exited the Physics building, stumbling down the stairs. She could hear Kerim and Harry calling her name as she ran out into the street. The air was heavy and humid and clung to her like a wet bathrobe. It was late in the evening and the sky was an angry purple. The moon was low in the sky, a crescent shape with a burnt orange color.

"Cristal, wait!" Kerim cried out, running toward her.

Something in his voice made her stop and turn to face him.

"Leave me alone."

He stopped in front of her. "We need to talk."

She looked past him to see if Harry was there. He wasn't. She shifted her eyes back onto Kerim, crossing her arms.

"Okay, explain to me how come when I'm near you, I feel like you are inside my head. And it seems you know what I'm feeling and thinking."

He took a deep breath and then looked away.

"So, are you going to tell me?" She stepped closer to him. "Or are you just going to stand there?"

"Okay, let's sit," he said, pointing to a bench a few feet away.

His voice was distant yet soft. His tone didn't exude its usual confidence.

He walked over, sat down, and placed one arm on the back of the bench. She followed him and sat on the far end of the bench. Maybe he wouldn't be able to read her mind if she created a larger expanse of space between them. She raised her chin slightly and focused her energy on watching his steel grey eyes.

"So, go ahead."

He began speaking, but his words were spoken so softly that she couldn't understand him. She inched closer and closer, straining to hear him. She realized at that moment that if she were to move any closer to him, she might end up in his lap.

He gave her a wicked grin but then tried to cover it up with his hand.

Oh, this guy is driving me nuts!

"Like I said before...I was in the Turkish Army serving as underground intelligence. I was trained to do a lot of things, one being, understanding and reading body language."

She tried to focus on his words.

"I can tell when someone is lying or if they are nervous," he continued. "I needed this for gathering intelligence for my covert missions. But when I left the Army, the skill was really useful with the ladies, if you know what I mean."

He made that statement as if it were a fact and nothing more.

She rolled her eyes, then stood up, and said, "Oh, please!"

Kerim reached out and grabbed her hand.

"Let me finish," he said, and pleaded with his eyes.

Cristal sank back down onto the bench. This was Kerim's last chance to explain himself. Patience was never her strong suit.

"I don't know what it is, but when I'm with you, I feel something more." He held her hand tight. "I can sense what you are feeling, especially when you are under stress."

She didn't know why she was still holding his hand. He looked down at her hand and released it from his grip.

"You mean like this?" she asked.

*So you **can** read my thoughts.*

"I sense what you feel. It's like you're sending me messages with your mind. Never in my life have I experienced something like this with anyone."

He spoke so differently from people she usually hung out with. He spoke in plain English—straight to the point and blunt. Not like the vague way Harry spoke to her. She closed her eyes and tried harder to take in what he was saying.

"Are you okay?" he asked.

She opened her eyes. "Yes, I'm fine. Just trying to process the info."

He patted her hand and gave her a small smile. "Do you believe in fate?" he asked.

"Not really. I hope you're not going to tell me you believe in destiny and all that crap."

Kerim raised his eyebrow. "Well, not really. But I was told that kismet or destiny would bring me to someone who would change my life."

He paused for a second as he searched for his words. "When I first met you, the word 'kismet' entered my head. Honestly, I don't know why." He looked into his hands.

Thoughts were swirling in Cristal's mind. Kerim had just admitted to hearing her thoughts. And now he's given her a bunch of stuff about them being destined to be together.

Kismet? I don't know what to say, she thought to herself.

Suddenly, a dark blue four-door sedan drove up, slowed down in front of them and then stopped. They both glanced up to see Harry sticking his head out from the passenger window. He had a crazed look on his face.

"Cristal, get in the car."

Who the hell does he think he is?

She could see Dr. Saeed was in the driver's seat. She stood up, clenching her fists while trying to keep her cool.

"Like I said, I'm not going to be part of your experiment anymore, Harry."

She shot a look at Kerim who was a few steps behind her. "Come on, Kerim. I want you to take me home."

Harry flung open the car door. He stepped onto the street, his intent gaze never moving away from Cristal. He walked up to her with long strides and stopped only when his face was inches away from hers.

"Get away from me, Harry," she said in a low whisper.

"You have to let me explain," he said.

Cristal couldn't believe her ears. Harry had a 200 IQ but the social skills of an ass.

"Explain what? Explain that you planned all of this, because you want to find your mother?" She jabbed her finger into his shoulder. "You never told me she was missing. And to think I thought we were friends."

She blinked her eyes hard, trying to stop the tears from coming.

Harry paced in front of her, like a black panther ready to pounce on his prey.

Kerim stood up from the bench. With Harry walking around her as if claiming her as his property, Kerim knew not to step inside the invisible circle.

Cristal pushed her thoughts towards his direction. *Kerim, please stay.*

He looked intently at her, affirming that he wasn't going anywhere without her.

Harry stopped and turned towards her. "There were times when

I thought about telling you about my mother. About everything, but..."

"But what?" The anger she was struggling to push down was wrapping its fingers around her heart.

"But nothing. I'm not very good at sharing. You know that about me." His voice sounded tired.

"Is that it? Are you serious? You used me for your experiment like one of Dr. Saeed's lab rats? I trusted you, Harry. How could you do this to me?"

The tears she didn't want to cry started burning her cheeks.

Harry didn't let down his guard. He was never good with expressing his feelings and she knew that. But knowing that wasn't enough. She had shared with him everything about herself—all of her deepest, darkest secrets and fears.

No more excuses from Harry. She waved to Kerim to come over. "Take me home."

He walked up to both of them. Harry stepped in front of her, giving Kerim a dirty look.

"Sorry, Harry," Kerim said, "but you got yourself into this on your own."

Cristal reached out for his hand. "Let's go. Where'd you park?"

Harry grabbed her by the arm. "No, you're not going anywhere."

She froze in her tracks. Harry Doubt wasn't a touchy feely kind of guy. For all the years she knew him, she never witnessed him even pat a guy on the back before.

"You can't stop her from going, Harry," Kerim said.

His words were respectful but firm.

Harry didn't move, but his hand squeezed her arm tighter.

"When I asked you to be a Truth Seeker," Harry said, "I never promised to tell you everything. You knew that and you accepted the invitation. I'm not going to apologize for not telling you about my mother. I didn't tell anyone about her."

His jawline was tense and his words were coming at her like sharp knives.

She tugged at her arm, trying to remove it from his grip. "I don't want to play your game anymore, Mr. Doubt," she said.

Her words revealed the bitterness she felt in her soul.

Harry stepped closer to her. His gaze was magnetic. His eyes were a deeper blue than she had ever recalled seeing before.

"It's not about me, or you, or any of us. And you know it. Your dad still communicates with you. You told me that yourself."

Her eyes widened. She glanced over to see Kerim's dark frown. Turning back, she could feel her heart pounding wildly against her chest wall.

"What does that have to do with anything?" she cried. The shrill tone in her voice could have broken glass. She looked over her shoulder to see Dr. Saeed standing with them.

"It has a lot to do with everything," Dr. Saeed said. "Your dad and all your friends' missing loved ones are trying to communicate. We need your help to find out what your dad and the others are trying to say."

PART II

NOTHING IS WHAT
IT SEEMS

A beacon bright in the blackness,
  Fragile sanity within all this madness.
  They fill her dish with love and
  Broken promises.

AR Vasquez

CHAPTER 13
LAND OF MILK AND HONEY

THE SUN WAS POURING into the musty hotel room. Cristal walked over and closed the shutters, which were made out of flimsy aluminum, the white paint peeling on the edges. They made little difference blocking out the blistering heat or the sounds of car horns blaring and the chatter from the street below. She had arrived in Tel Aviv ten days earlier, but she still could not adjust to the climate or the culture.

The days were blurred with meetings at the GN office in Haifa in the day and mission meetings with Harry, Dr. Saeed, Gabriel, Kerim, and Rinaldo at night. After the earthquake one week earlier, many GN computer networks had a melt down. Harry used the opportunity to get a temporary transfer for Cristal and himself to the GN Haifa office citing that the data that she had recovered all point to Israel being the location where their missing family were being held. Dr. Saeed must have made arrangements, too, because he arrived a few days after they did.

She could have pretended that she was vacationing, if she wasn't staying in a shabby two-star hotel where the only good feature was that it was close to the Bograshov Beach and restaurants. Global Nation proudly stated at their regular all-staff meetings that they did not misuse their donors' funds for unnecessary travel expenses. Of course, that same rule didn't seem to apply to senior management. She recalled how her senior manager, George Beaver once bragged that when he went with Lionheart to a convention in Brazil, they had stayed at a "Five Star All-Inclusive Resort."

Her room was on the fourth floor and was modestly furnished. It had a queen-sized bed with a mattress that had a huge depressive dent in the middle with wired springs that jabbed into her back when she slept. Two wooden chairs were positioned by the window that looked like they were held together with rubber bands. The other furniture included a wooden side table and a small twenty-four-inch old style Cathode ray tube television that sat on a metal bracket hung from the ceiling in the corner of the room.

Although she had a "non-smoking" room, she spent the first morning "airing out" the room to get rid of the cigarette smoke stench. And despite the fact there was an air conditioner, she preferred to keep it off, because instead of the box spewing out cold air, it filled the room with smelly dank air. To top it all off, the bathroom was so small that she could do her makeup, have a shower and sit on the toilet all at the same time.

She spent the first day by herself staring at the worn marble tiled floor and at the walls with their ugly strokes of lumpy plaster covered with salmon-colored paint.

Instead of staying at the same hotel, Harry had decided to camp out with his aunt who lived fifteen minutes away. He had told them that he needed to connect with his family in order to help them with their missions.

Kerim had been busy arranging accommodations for Gabriel and himself. He found an ex-military friend who lived close to the hotel, which left Cristal by herself in her miserable room.

To pass time, she flipped through the photos on her cell phone, and stopped to enlarge a photo of Kerim where he was smiling at her and his fingers gestured a peace sign. The photo was taken onboard the flight to Israel.

⚜

IT HAD BEEN her first international flight on a Boeing 747 across the ocean. It started out horribly. The plane was full of screaming kids and crying babies. Thankfully, Kerim and Gabriel were on the same flight, although they were seated in different rows.

Her seat number had been F29, the middle row in front of a wall with a toddler on her left who spent most of the trip wailing at the top of her lungs. The child's mother who was seated on the other side of the girl had put earplugs in and covered her eyes with an eye mask. Cristal couldn't believe how she could ignore her own child who obviously was frightened and uncomfortable. She tried to talk to the little girl in an effort to comfort her. But the girl only reacted by screaming louder.

So much for trying to be a Good Samaritan.

On her right side sat an unsociable woman, probably in her early forties with dark hair, cut short. Sitting like a queen on her throne, her elbow hung over the arm rest between them, digging into Cristal's side. She was what Kerim described later as a "full-bodied woman" referring to her wide hips and generous-sized bosom. The woman had eyed Cristal carefully, her lips pursed together as if she had just eaten a bucket of lemons.

Get a life, she remembered thinking to herself.

When she gave up all hope of having any rest on the flight, Kerim had suddenly appeared in the aisle. He looked over at her and gave her a wink.

What is he doing? Harry had told all of us to be inconspicuous.

The woman who had been flipping through a beauty magazine

81

glanced up to look at him. Cristal noticed that her grim face melted and her pursed lips turned into a warm glowing smile.

Kerim, you have the power to melt glaciers.

Kerim began speaking in a language that Cristal guessed was Hebrew, given that the flight was a direct flight to Tel Aviv and over 60 percent of the passengers were Israelis returning home from their holidays in New York. The other 20 percent were New Yorkers who apparently had dual Israeli citizenship. This is what Kerim had mentioned to her while waiting at the airport before boarding the plane.

Although Cristal couldn't understand what they were saying, she knew Kerim was doing what he was good at—charming the lady and making her giggle like a schoolgirl. Kerim pointed towards Cristal and said something that caused the lady to burst out into peals of laughter.

What the heck?

His hands then waved towards his seat at the back of the plane.

Still giggling, the lady nodded her head, grabbed her things and stood up, her fat bottom brushing against Cristal's arm. She glanced down and offered Cristal an apologetic smile before turning back to Kerim. He offered his hand to help as she squeezed herself out of the row into the aisle.

"*Shalom*, handsome. I will see you in the land of milk and honey," the woman said, purring like a cat, as if in an attempt to sound sultry, but instead, it reminded Cristal of a squawking seagull.

Cristal rolled her eyes, trying her best to contain her laughter. The woman waddled away, swaying her hips. She glanced back at Kerim, blowing him a kiss.

Oh, how sweet.

When the woman was far from sight, Kerim eased himself into the recently vacated seat. He slipped his messenger bag under the seat in front of him and leaned back with a boyish grin on his face.

"What was that all about?" Cristal asked, looking at the aisle where the lady had said her good-byes.

He smirked.

"My skills come in quite handy in these types of situations."

Before she could respond, he reclined his seat and closed his eyes. She sighed and resigned herself to not ask any further questions.

You are a funny character, Kerim Ilgaz.

Taking his lead, she reclined her seat and closed her eyes. Maybe a snooze would help her relax.

Nine hours left and counting, she thought to herself.

❦

LESS THAN AN HOUR LATER, she opened her eyes. Sleep had not come, despite all her efforts. The little girl beside her had thankfully cried herself to sleep. Her parents now were chattering to each other loudly across the other aisle in their language, while shoving nuts into their faces.

Cristal's ears were picking up many conversations in multiple languages around her. The sounds seemed to be increasing in volume, hurting her ears. For some reason, words spoken in other languages always seemed to magnify in her ears, reverberating in her skull. The worst part was that no matter how hard she tried to understand the meaning of the words, her brain drew a blank slate that caused her to become even more frustrated.

"Hey, what's the matter? Can't sleep?" Kerim asked.

She grumbled, "I have a headache."

She turned her head away from him. How could she tell him about her bizarre problem?

CHAPTER 14
IN MY HEAD

D URING HER FIRST YEAR as an undergraduate at GN University, Cristal had decided to take a class in introductory Spanish hoping to help improve her communication skills with gamers in Spanish-speaking countries like Mexico and Spain. Truth be told, she was envious with the fact that Harry had taught himself five different languages. He told her that it helped give him the advantage when playing with Truth Seekers from around the world. She was confident that she could master the language in a few weeks, given the fact she was able to read at super speeds.

Two months later, no matter how fast she was able to read through the textbooks, the words never stuck in her head. When she tried to form the words with her mouth, she couldn't remember what the words were. It was one of her greatest weaknesses, which she never could overcome.

"Do you need help?" Ms. Cruz, her Spanish professor asked her.

She must have been surprised to see Cristal struggling. How could Cristal Hernandez, an Honors student have problems in Introducción al Español 100?

"Come to my classroom every day after school. I can help."

Cristal was grateful and accepted her offer willingly.

Unfortunately, after three lessons, even Ms. Cruz had to admit that there was no hope for Cristal. She dropped out of the class soon after.

Cristal never mentioned this to anyone. Not to her mother. Not to Harry.

When other students asked her why she dropped the class, she simply said, "Spanish sucks."

Soon afterwards, something strange began happening to her. She found that when she was in a crowd of people who were speaking in another language, the sound would increase like a muddle of voices in her head—all shouting to be heard. She would cup her hands over her ears and run away to get the voices out of her head. Over time, she was able to control the "situation" by putting on her headset and drowning out the sound with music. Not just any music. Her carefully selected assortment of songs stored on her cell phone was the only way she could block out the noise.

ON THE PLANE ride to Tel Aviv, the voices of the passengers were getting louder and louder in her head. She glanced over at Kerim who was busy watching a movie on the screen in front of him. She reached into her bag on the floor, rummaging for her phone. *Where in the world did I put it?*

"Looking for this?"

Dangling in front of her was her cellphone. Kerim had a mischievous grin as he handed it to her.

"Very funny," she said, grabbing the phone from his hand.

"So what kind of music do you listen to?" he whispered in her ear.

She flashed him a disarming smile.

"Sir, like I said earlier, I'm not interested in small talk."

His eyebrows shot up and he shook his head as he chuckled into his hand. She smiled to herself as she shoved the ear buds into her ears and then hit the play button on her phone's music player.

She could see Kerim was still talking, but she let the beat of the music from one of her favorite alternative bands, *Bittersweetness*, drown out his voice and all the other voices in her head.

Kill this desire to fly
close to the sun, burning wing tips,
singe away the feathers
Can this hollowness be filled
Forgiveness: another feather to fall from wing...

"I like that song, too," she heard Kerim say as his voice entered her head.

She opened her eyes. Kerim's eyes were closed, but he had a smile on his face.

She shook her head and shut her eyes. Her mind was playing tricks on her.

"No, it's not."

Her eyes sprung open and she sat upright, turning her body toward Kerim.

"Did you say something?"

He opened one eye, pointed to himself and said, "Who me?"

She lowered the volume on her phone.

"You know what I'm talking about."

Kerim sat up and turned to face her.

"Cristal, are you okay?" he asked.

She took a deep breath, holding back the desire to scream at him.

"I'm not going to say it again. What are you doing to me?"

He stared at her blankly, and for a moment, she doubted herself.

Shaking her head, she said, "Never mind. I'm just tired. Sorry to bug you."

Closing her eyes, she reached for her phone and turned up the volume.

"*I can help you,*" Kerim's voice said in her head.

She opened one eye and saw Kerim was leaning back with his eyes closed. There was a smile on his face, and she swore she could see it getting wider.

"Help me what?" she said out loud.

"*Get over the problem you have with learning another language,*" he said, still in her head.

What? Now how did he know that? She knew he was able to sense things about her, but how in the world would he be able to sense she had a problem with languages? And how come she could hear him in her mind?

"*It just started when you had your eyes closed earlier, Cristal,*" his voice in her head said. "*I could hear your thoughts. They weren't clear, but the more upset you became, the clearer they were.*"

"Okay, that only half answers my questions. How in the world are you talking to me in my head?"

"*Not sure, but I think when you started listening to your music, I could hear it, too,*" his voice said. "*And for some reason, through the music, I felt I could reach you. The feeling was so strong that I sang the message to you in my head.* "

He sat up turning to her, his mesmerizing eyes gazing deep into hers.

"And you heard me...didn't you?" he asked her.

Her heart started beating harder, her breathing faster. Everything around her started spinning. Kerim grabbed her hand.

"Breathe, Cristal, breathe."

She felt her hands shaking. *Oh no!* The plane started rocking violently. Screams from the passengers filled the cabin. *No, please don't let this happen again.* Tears streaked down her cheeks as she imagined the worst thing that would happen next.

Kerim held her hand tight and pulled her towards him. She glanced up to see his lips so close to her face.

"Everything is going to be fine, Cristal," he whispered, stroking her hair.

She could smell his scent in her nostrils. Her body felt magnetic energy move from inside her towards him.

Kerim pulled her tighter into his embrace. Before she could push him away or say anything, his head bent down and his mouth pressed down on hers. She felt her body flush with excitement as she melted into his kiss. Her hand was on his chest, and she could feel his heart beating hard. Her other hand found its way to his wavy hair. Pulling a handful gently into her hands, she marveled at how soft it felt in her fingers. Suspended in the first kiss, tongues searching each other, their hands explored each other's body. While enjoying the moment, a part of her suddenly realized that the plane had stopped shaking. She opened her eyes and looked to see the flight attendants were running around.

"The plane just passed through a small batch of turbulence. Everything is fine," the Asian flight attendant said to them as she rushed by.

She looked over at Kerim. His eyes were warm and dreamy; his smile was relaxed, and his face seemed to have an afterglow. It was then that she picked up her cell phone, and pointed the camera lens at him.

"I want to keep the way you're looking at me now in my memory forever," she whispered.

He tilted his head and raised his fingers in the "peace" sign, the pointer and middle fingers up.

"Actually, it means *victory*," he said as she snapped the photo.

She liked that it could mean both peace and victory.

She cuddled up close to him and slept for the rest of the flight, listening to the songs on her phone with Kerim's voice singing along in her head.

CHAPTER 15

CALM BEFORE THE STORM

KERIM WAS MEETING HER in the hotel lobby soon. It was their first full day off since they arrived, and he had promised to show her around.

The first few days going to the Global Nation office in Haifa was awkward to say the least. Every morning at 7:00 a.m., like an alarm clock, Harry waited in a small silver Subaru hatchback, outside the hotel—never a minute late. Although it was annoying, she was comforted knowing he would be there. Life was different here. Not that it was a bad thing. It was difficult for her not being able to speak or understand the language. Hotel workers were generally polite.

"How are you, Miss? Do you need anything, Miss?" they would say, always with their well-rehearsed smiles.

But if she wanted something, an extra towel or bar of soap, suddenly no one could understand English.

EVERY NIGHT, Kerim patiently tried to teach her conversational

Hebrew and Arabic. His creative teaching style using music was experimental, but she had to admit that it was working. The only phrase she was able to say in both languages was "Ayph hshyrvtym?" and "Wayne hamam?" which meant, "Where is the washroom?"

"Well, at least I will never worry about you finding a bathroom," he teased her.

She smacked his shoulder playfully.

During the day, she and Harry were supposedly restoring the server networks at GN, but in reality, they were downloading data for Cristal to decode. If it were all about work, she wouldn't have minded so much. The problem was that Harry was always trying to corner her.

"There are things I wish I could share with you," he said, searching her eyes, hoping to see the old Cristal, the one who used to be willing to listen.

That wasn't going to happen.

"Let's keep things professional, Harry," she said, refusing to let him get an inch closer to her. "We're here to do a job, so let me do my work."

He grabbed her elbow, pulling her to him.

"You know I care about you," he whispered into her hair.

Her mind was telling her to push him away, but her body froze.

"I always have," he said, releasing his grip.

He turned away and left her feeling confused and empty.

If that weren't enough, Dr. Saeed was beginning to give her the creeps. He would sneak questions into their conversations, like: "Have you been sleeping well? Have you had any other fainting spells? Do you want to talk about the visions you've had?"

How she wanted to tell him—*Leave me alone! I'm not your lab rat.* But she bit her tongue, trying to keep things polite.

She wished she could be with Kerim and Gabriel instead of being stuck at the GN office. Harry had sent them on missions in Haifa and Gaza to meet with other Truth Seekers.

"I want to go with them to meet the others," she told Harry.

"No, we need you here at GN. We can't let the New York office suspect what we are doing," he said.

His tone was sharp and authoritative.

"You're the boss," she mumbled under her breath.

In the evenings, Harry asked all of them to meet to discuss the missions. Cristal made sure to sit beside Kerim. He could speak to her inside her head while she had one ear bud in her ear, listening to her music.

"I'll take you back to your hotel after work," Kerim's voice told her.

"You promise to tell me everything you uncovered today in Gaza?" she responded.

"After I teach you a few more phrases in Hebrew and Arabic." He turned to her and winked. *"Like, I love you, my sweetheart."*

Her cheeks turned several shades of red. *Did he say that out loud?* She calmed down when she saw that everyone was focused on Harry at the front of the room. Harry's eyes seemed to bore into hers. He was talking to everyone, but he seemed to only be looking at her.

"I wish we could sneak out of here," she said in her thoughts.

"Patience, my dear Cristal. Let's save the world first and then we can go play."

She glanced over at Kerim who reached over and squeezed her knee.

Silent conversations—it was weird, but romantic. Most importantly, it was their little secret.

THE HOTEL PHONE RANG, startling her from her thoughts. She glanced at her watch as she picked up the phone. Kerim must be in the lobby now.

"Kerim, I'm on my way down."

A deep voice responded, but it wasn't Kerim's.

"Ms. Hernandez, this is the hotel concierge. There is an I.S. agent here who wants to speak with you."

Why would a security agent want to speak with me?

"Madame, are you still there?"

She shook her head to clear her thoughts.

"Yes, I am coming down."

CHAPTER 16
JOANNA MAKES PLANS

Zero: The data you sent this morning should have been encrypted.

Onyx: It's been crazy here. Elf man is riding my back and now I have to do the reports for our whole team. Thanks a lot for leaving me behind.

Zero: We need you over there. You're one of the best programmers on our team. We're counting on you to get the data we need.

Joanna was about to type something sarcastic, but paused.

Zero: I am personally counting on you.

Before responding, she thought to herself, Oh, really? You think I'm that stupid to believe that crap?

Zero: I'll contact you again in 10 hours. SYL

OMG. Seriously? She wasn't going to let Harry get away with this.

She finished typing an email and sent it to her friend, Jenna

Adams, a journalist for the *New York Times*. You wait and see who should have gone to Tel Aviv with you, Harry, she thought to herself.

"Joanna, are you on planet Earth?"

Beaver, the Elf man, was standing at her cubicle. Just the sight of him made her want to barf. Everyone on the IT team knew he was a useless dweeb. He wore his senior manager title as if it were his shield that would protect him from the truth.

She rolled her eyes.

"What do you want, Beaver?"

She turned back to her screen.

"Shelley wants to see you," he said with a sly smile.

Freak! What does the boss want to see me about? Why did Harry leave me here to hold down the fort all by myself?

"Did you hear me? She's waiting for you."

He turned away, waving his hand as if he was summoning his pet Schnauzer. Her hand tightened around her mouse as she imagined hurling it right between Beaver's beady brown eyes.

He turned his head around and mouthed to her, "Well, are you coming?"

She pushed her chair back, stood up and walked towards him, trying hard not to make a face. He pointed to his watch with his "hurry up" face and let out an exasperated sigh, which sounded like air coming out of his rear. Ugh! She let him walk ahead of her. His royal "highneyness" was enjoying having his minion follow three steps behind.

Her cell phone vibrated inside her pocket. It was a text message from Jenna.

Jenna: Hey, Joanna, got your email. What's up?
Joanna: You asked me about Harry Doubt. Have a story about his close friends.
Jenna: Finally came to your senses, girl? Come over after work. You still like sushi?

Joanna: See you @ 6. Will bring drinks.

A smile crept onto her face. She shoved her phone back in her pocket.

⁂

HARRY DOUBT, the icon of alternate reality game creators was a private guy. Gamers could only play by his personal invitation. Joanna, who had been playing obsessively on Truth Seekers every night, took the job at Global Nation at the GN University campus in New York City when Harry sent out the following message via the Truth Seekers' private message system:

"Looking for a real Truth Seekers' mission? Only inviting 5 of the top gamers here. You'll get to work closely with me on missions which are yet to be disclosed."

Joanna didn't think twice. At twenty-four years old and a recent graduate of the Emery College's Game Art and Design Program in San José, California, she was itching to do something fun. She bought a one-way ticket to New York City.

His father, Aaron Doub, professor of theoretical physics at Global Nation University of New York, was intelligent and entertaining without even trying to be. People paid big dollars to watch him guest speak at conferences. He introduced himself as a "futurist" and a "mad scientist." His quirky habits were his signature. Constantly he'd push his black, horn-rimmed glasses up on the bridge of his beak-like nose, and wave his hands around excitedly, explaining a breakthrough in something unheard of, like worm holes. He wore a T-shirt that said, "I'm from 2025." His presentations were captured on thousands of YouTube videos, which Truth Seekers shared on discussion forums. Too bad he died so suddenly. Harry must have been so devastated to lose such an ingenious father.

❦

THEY WERE POLISHING off the contents of their Bento boxes while sitting around the coffee table, cross-legged on the floor—like the good old days. She watched Jenna clearing up the empty food containers and bringing them to the kitchen. She would have offered to help, but why bother?

She smirked to herself observing how Jenna's apartment was small and cramped compared to hers. It made her remember how she had negotiated with Harry to get her a two-bedroom, fully furnished apartment with minimum 900 square footage and the lease paid in full for a year. It was her way to test him to see how much of a valuable asset he thought she was to the team. When she had arrived in New York, not only did he hold up his end of the bargain, he managed to get her a luxury suite on Crosby Street in Soho. She knew that compared to the other Truth Seekers in NYC, her place was in the best location, had the best layout, and had the coolest furniture.

Jenna returned with two wine glasses and the bottle of red wine that Joanna had brought earlier.

"Sushi was just what I was craving. Thanks again, Jenna."

"My pleasure. It wasn't much. Just spent all afternoon making them for you. Not!" she laughed, tossing her bleach blonde hair to the side. "Let's get to work."

She flipped open her laptop.

Joanna smiled to herself. Jenna was never one to mince words. She always had been driven, even when they were college room-mates. Jenna was a California babe—blonde, blue eyes, and hot "bod" with brains to top it off. Added to the mix were her cold tactics that she used to get her way, even if it meant sleeping with whomever she needed to get the story. Together, Joanna and Jenna, were a formidable pair.

DOUBT

"So give me the goods, Joanna," she said with her usual, "I'm losing my patience" tone.

"Shut up and start typing," Joanna replied.

Jenna never intimidated her, *New York Times* journalist or not.

Jenna smiled, flashing her perfect white teeth.

"Webcam will get everything I need. Now take a sip and start talking."

Jenna saluted her with her wine glass, kicked off her heels and curled up on the couch.

"Cristal Hernandez and Kerim Ilgaz. They're Harry's prized Truth Seekers. But that's not the story."

She paused.

"Come on, what is it?" Jenna moved forward on the edge of the couch.

"I think that Cristal was responsible for starting the earthquake that happened in different countries all over the world. And I think Kerim had something to do with it, too."

Jenna rolled her eyes and closed her laptop.

"You've really lost it, Joanna. I can't believe I wasted my evening waiting for this earth shattering information."

She stood up and started putting away her things.

"I'm a serious journalist. I don't do gossip or ET stories."

"Fine. Don't believe me," Joanna said and grabbed her purse from the coffee table. "But I saw it myself with my own eyes."

"Wait," Jenna said and turned to look at her. "What do you mean?"

"Aren't you going to record what I tell you?" Joanna asked.

"No, not until I'm sure it's worth it," Jenna said, while leaning back and waiting. "And the only reason I'm willing to hear any of this psycho-babble is the fact it's coming from you. So thrill me."

"Harry and I were meeting with Cristal, Kerim, and Gabriel on video chat the day of the earthquake. At the precise time it happened, I saw Cristal freeze, almost like a zombie. Her eyes were blank, while the whole room was shaking like crazy. Kerim was in the doorway, holding onto the doorframe and Gabriel was holding onto him with his eyes closed."

She closed her eyes trying to remember what she saw that day.

"The weird thing was Cristal and Kerim were staring at each other. They both were real calm during the whole thing. Then the screen went black."

She opened her eyes to see Jenna's "whatever" expression on her face.

"Great, Joanna," Jenna said rolling her eyes again. "Now, I am really convinced."

Joanna could not ignore the thick layer of sarcasm in her friend's voice. She sat back down and took out her smart phone. She opened up a video and maximized it on the screen.

"Here. Watch this," she said, handing her phone to Jenna.

Jenna sighed and took it from her hand.

"This better be good," she said.

The video started playing. The screen filled with the larger-than-life image of Shelley Lionheart, wearing a neon-white suit, seated at her glass desk in her white high-back leather office chair in her fifteen-foot windowed penthouse office. The picture jittered slightly —Joanna had done her best to keep her phone steady.

"You're doing an exceptional job filling in for Harry and Cristal," Shelley was saying.

"Thanks, I'm just doing my job," she heard herself say.

Shelley leaned forward, crossing her hands on the desk. Her two-inch nails were painted the shade of blood red. It took a lot for Joanna to be intimidated, but she had to admit that being in the presence of Shelley Lionheart made her a bit squeamish.

"This information must stay in this room," Lionheart said, lowering her voice. "Can I trust you to keep confidential information?"

"Umm, yes, of course. I'm a professional," Joanna replied, a little too fast.

"We both know that George Beaver is an incompetent programmer and senior manager," Shelley continued. "I need someone like you at my side to keep me abreast of what is happening in our IT systems—from current software installations, to development roadmaps and security concerns."

Shelley smiled, if you could call it a smile. It appeared more like a sneer.

Joanna remembered how excited she should have felt. Finally, someone from the top was recognizing her potential. But part of her felt weird—like she was just about to sell her soul to the devil. She shivered at the thought. *Now where did that crazy idea come from?*

The picture shifted slightly as Shelley rose from her chair. The word *rose* was the best way to describe it. Her body seemed to glide upwards as she stood. It could have been the resolution of the video, but Shelley seemed to become transparent just for a second before she walked (glided) around the desk to stand in front of her.

The picture shifted abruptly and the screen was filled with a blurred image.

The sound was clearer now with Shelley's voice closer to the phone.

"We have some information about illicit activity from one of our professors at the GN University. His name is Dr. Nariman, but students refer to him as Dr. Saeed. It seems he accessed encrypted files in our restricted server with the help of some of your colleagues. I want you to find any trace of suspicious activity in the logs, and see if you can track its sources to identify the hackers. This will be done under the guise of a "scheduled overhaul" of our developer systems to update our server software and rebuild our databases. You will be in charge. This is high-level priority, and I'll make sure Beaver stays out of your way. We'll call this project "System overhaul." I don't want you to let anyone know what the real purpose of this project is. Do you understand, Ms. Chan?"

The video shook slightly as Joanna shifted her weight.

"Yes, I understand."

"Good. If I am pleased with your report, we'll see about giving you a promotion. Maybe you can take Beaver's job."

The video shook again as she stood up.

"Thank you, Shelley. I really appreciate it," she heard herself saying.

Ugh, it almost sounded like she was gushing all over her.

The video ended abruptly.

Jenna looked up from the phone and stared at her, a smile stretching across her face.

"Okay, Joanna, I'm down with corporate espionage. You may have something. Not sure what it is yet, but I am going to start digging."

Joanna pursed her lips together while her fingers fidgeted with a strand of her hair.

"Do you need anything from me?" Joanna asked.

"Oh, yeah," Jenna said, almost gleefully. "You're going to give me everything you know about Harry, Cristal, and Kerim. Every time Shelley talks to you, you're going to let me know a.s.a.p."

"Sounds fine," Joanna replied.

She should have been happy, but something was nagging at her— telling her to stop.

"And before I forget, I need two things from you," Jenna added. "One, before you tell me about Cristal causing an earthquake and shining lights, you need to show me some proof. And two, I want you to get me into the Truth Seekers."

"What? You a Truth Seeker?"

Joanna burst out laughing. *Did she think it was going to be that easy?*

"Yeah," Jenna said, as she started typing, searching online.

She had already started mining the Internet for the data. She knew this would be one of her best *New York Times* articles ever.

"And I want to know where Harry is. I'm going to get to the source as soon as possible."

"You can't join the Truth Seekers. You don't even play video games. And it's all by invitation only. Harry invites only the top players. Do you really need to be a Truth Seeker to get what you need?"

Joanna's stomach started turning. The sushi was playing havoc with her intestines.

"Do you really need me to answer that question?" Jenna said, looking into the distance, as if analyzing the situation and considering all her options.

Joanna sat back, trying to think as well. But her thoughts were wandering away. She knew she just betrayed the Truth Seekers. More importantly, she understood now she had just started something. Exactly what, she didn't know.

CHAPTER 17
AGENT IS WATCHING

CRISTAL SAW A COUPLE OF tourists at the hotel counter arguing with the concierge. She scanned the lobby and noticed two boys who looked like they were local, hanging around the American girls who were apparently staying at the hotel. A stout man dressed in a black suit with sunglasses was seated in a chair near the front door of the lobby. He was watching her carefully. *That must be the security agent who asked to see me.*

She took her time walking over to the counter, grateful that the concierge was busy with the tourists. It would give Harry enough time to get there and assist with the interrogation.

She had texted him immediately after receiving the phone call, "Urgent. Get here ASAP. Agent in lobby wants to question me."

His response was, "Stall until I get there."

From the corner of her eye, she could see that the agent had stood up. He was walking towards her.

"Ms. Hernandez," a woman's voice called from behind her.

Cristal turned, expecting to see someone from the hotel staff.

"Yes?"

Standing in front of her was the full-bodied woman who had sat beside her on the airplane. *What was she doing here?*

The woman was holding up her identification, which read, "Yaffa Bauer, National Security Agent." The photo on the ID displayed an expressionless version of the woman.

"My name Yaffa," she said, putting her ID into her pocket. "You remember me?"

Cristal couldn't figure out what this lady was doing here.

"Sorry, but what do you want from me?"

Yaffa Bauer motioned for her to follow her to a room off the side of the hotel counter.

"We talk in private," Yaffa replied loudly with a strong Hebrew accent.

Cristal glanced over to the hotel entrance, relieved to see Harry walking inside. She noticed that since he had come to Tel Aviv that his looks had changed somewhat. Perhaps it was the Middle Eastern sun that painted his hair with gold highlights and warmed his skin color from a pale white to a copper bronze. Was it the same sun that made his blue eyes appear bluer and deeper than the ocean?

"Ms. Hernandez," Yaffa prompted, as if impatient with the delay.

"Just a minute. My boss is here. Can he join us?" Cristal asked.

Yaffa turned to look at Harry who now stood beside them. Cristal noticed that Harry was much taller than the agent. Yaffa had to stretch her neck to look up at him. Quickly, as if on cue, Yaffa put her pudgy arms on her wide hips and glared at Harry.

"Shalom," Harry said, stretching his hand out to shake her hand.

The agent gave Harry a quick nod in acknowledgment of his greeting. She eyed him suspiciously and then shifted her attention to Cristal.

"Better we speak alone," she said in a firm voice.

Cristal crossed her arms over her chest.

"Have I done anything wrong?"

Yaffa's nostrils flared slightly before she responded, glancing briefly at Harry.

"No, I have questions."

Harry said, "Do you have a warrant?"

He stepped closer to Yaffa.

"No, no warrant," she sneered. "This is Israel, not episode of *Law & Order*."

Harry chuckled. He responded to her switching from English to Hebrew. His voice had softened as he reached into his back pocket to take out his wallet. He showed her his Israeli ID. Yaffa took a look and nodded her head, her body relaxing as she listened. They spoke with each other in Hebrew for a few minutes, while Cristal stood and watched.

Yaffa began to smile as she faced Cristal, and said in broken English, "Okay, we speak like friends then. Just tell me the truth."

She motioned to the people sitting in the lobby chairs to get up, at the same time that she flashed her ID at them. The man and woman looked at each other, obviously frightened that an agent was in their presence. They quickly gathered their things, got up, and left.

"Sit," she said as she sank down onto the couch.

She flashed a dirty look at another couple who were about to sit beside her. When they ignored her, she waved her ID at them. They apologized in hushed voices and walked away.

Cristal glanced at Harry, unsure of what to do next. Harry gave her a small and comforting smile.

Yaffa opened her handbag and rummaged about until she pulled out her smartphone. She swiped the screen and tapped icons before turning the phone towards them.

On the screen was a photo of the inside of an airplane. The people visible in the photo were screaming, as if fearing for their lives. Cristal felt Harry's hand cover hers. Her stomach was twisting into knots.

Yaffa swiped the screen to display another photo. In this one, Kerim was reclined in his seat, and Cristal's head was resting on his shoulder. Cristal bit her bottom lip, wondering what Harry was thinking.

"Look closer," Yaffa said as she pinched the screen, zooming into a close-up of Kerim's head.

As the photo sharpened, Cristal saw something odd. Surrounding Kerim's head was a soft white glow, almost like an aura. Were her eyes playing tricks on her?

"Who is this man?" Yaffa asked.

Cristal cleared her throat before answering, and replied, "That's Kerim Ilgaz."

"How you know him?" Yaffa inquired.

Cristal paused. Her insides were shaking. Part of her was afraid to lose control and cause another *event*.

She managed to say, "Kerim is a subcontractor that Harry hired. Maybe you should ask Harry."

"Ah, yes, Harry told me. Excuse, my English is not so good. I want to know who is Kerim to you? Lover?"

"What?" Cristal asked, trying her best not to sound defensive.

Yaffa pursed her lips, and her nostrils flared even more than before, as she said, "We were on same flight. Two of us agents are always on flights from New York to Tel Aviv. After the plane stop shaking, I check to see that passengers are safe. When I come back, I saw you with this man. I took the picture. Submitted it with report."

Cristal crossed her arms. *She is driving me nuts.*

"I still don't know what the issue is."

"You see the halo around him?" Yaffa said gruffly.

Harry took the phone from her hand and examined the picture more carefully.

"Very good Photoshop job, Yaffa," he said with a grin.

"Hmph!" Yaffa snorted and grabbed the phone back.

"This is photo I took. No Photoshop."

She swiped the screen quickly and more photos of Kerim and Cristal flashed before them. The same weird light was around Kerim's head in each photo. The last one was a video. Yaffa tapped the "Play" button.

In the video, the glow surrounding Kerim's head was more obvious. Harry's gaze met Cristal's briefly. Yaffa snorted, pleased that she had finally gotten the attention of both Cristal and Harry.

"So, you want to answer my questions now?" she asked, facing Cristal.

Her other hand waved for Harry to keep his mouth shut.

"Kerim is a friend, a good friend. It was my first time flying on an international flight. He was helping me relax and keep calm." *It was true.*

Yaffa scribbled notes in her notepad, while mumbling to herself, "Hmph...friend."

Cristal looked at Yaffa sideways and asked, "Why do you say *friend* that way? It's like you don't believe me!"

Yaffa's pea green eyes met hers. Her smile widened, which pushed her chipmunk cheeks aside.

"When Ilgaz asked me to give my seat to him, he tell me you are his half-sister and you are afraid to fly in airplanes."

Cristal choked back her laughter.

"I'm not laughing at your English, Yaffa, really. I'm not good at languages. But I think Kerim pulled a fast one on you. Maybe he thought you would give up your seat if you thought we were brother and sister."

Yaffa's eyebrows raised as she spoke.

"Ah...is that so?"

She scribbled again in her notepad. Putting down her pen, she raised her head and focused her eyes on Cristal.

"Okay, I want to know more about Kerim. Who he is, his past, who his friends are, and why he is in Israel. From our investigation, we do not have much information on Kerim Ilgaz before 2009. No family, no friends, no lovers, no work history, *shvm dbr*—nothing."

Harry said, "I told you everything about Kerim. He is here as a subcontractor for Global Nation. He provides security for Cristal, myself, and the staff at the GN office in Haifa. You can check this with our head office. Cristal does not know much about him because I was the one who hired him."

Yaffa sighed, giving him a polite smile before standing up.

"Yes, yes, you tell me this. It is time now for me to go. Take my information. You remember more, contact me. Like I tell Harry in Hebrew, Kerim Ilgaz is considered threat to national security. Here, we say someone is guilty until he proves he is innocent."

She gave them a grunt and then motioned to the other agents who were scattered around the lobby that it was time to leave. Harry gave Yaffa a smile, tapping Cristal on the foot to signal for her to do the same. Cristal gave her a forced smile. Yaffa returned the fake smile, turned around and walked towards the hotel entrance, the agents tailing behind her. She glanced over her shoulder briefly before leaving the hotel.

"Shalom," she said before walking out the door.

CHAPTER 18

WHAT NEXT?

HARRY PACED BACK AND FORTH in front of her. He glanced at his watch while mumbling under his breath.

"Sit down," Cristal demanded, pointing to the chair beside her. "You're making me nervous."

"I'm trying to figure out what to do next," he said quietly.

"Kerim is going to be here soon," Cristal stated in a matter-of-fact way. "Are you going to tell him what happened?"

Harry whirled around and pointed a finger at her.

"Don't say a word! You got that, Cristal? Until we find out more about him, consider him a hostile."

Cristal couldn't believe her ears. She leapt out of her chair, and stood facing him eye-to-eye, as if daring him to challenge her.

"Hostile? This isn't a game, Harry. You said you checked him out before inviting him to the Truth Seekers. Just because some crazy agent shows us some weird photos, now you think that Kerim is a hostile?"

Her voice echoed in the lobby.

She followed Harry's gaze to see where he was looking. She noted that he was peering at the main entrance of the hotel. She sucked in her breath and gasped when she saw Kerim standing between the opened glass doors. His olive-colored skin contrasted his white unbuttoned long sleeve shirt and black jeans. But what made her hold her breath was the bright blinding light that blazed around him like angry flames.

He moved away from the door, and the light behind him flooded into the lobby. She realized that the setting sun had played optical tricks on her. Or so she thought.

He stood motionless.

"Kerim," she called out, walking over to him.

He looked past her, as if not seeing her. His grey eyes were fixed on Harry.

"What's this about?" he asked.

Harry moved in closer, but he didn't volunteer a response. Cristal sighed, knowing that she would have to be the first person to speak.

"An agent was here asking questions about you," Cristal said.

The heat from Harry's glare could have disintegrated steel.

"Agent?" Kerim asked.

"Let's go somewhere else to talk," Harry demanded, glancing at the group of hotel guests that were entering the lobby.

"Sorry," Kerim announced, "but I'm not going anywhere with anyone who thinks I'm the enemy."

His jawline was tense, his voice quiet. He gave Cristal a look.

She reached out for his arm. He pulled it away from her, turned and walked back towards the hotel entrance. The doors opened and he marched outside onto the street towards his motorbike.

"Kerim, please," she called out in a loud voice, while running after him.

"Cristal, let him go," she heard Harry say as he followed behind her.

"Leave me alone, Harry," she snapped.

Kerim was already on his bike with the engine roaring.

"Wait for me, please!" *You can't leave me here.*

Kerim turned around and looked at her. His eyes met hers.

Please, don't leave me here.

He paused for a moment and then tilted his head for her to climb on. Without hesitation, she grabbed his shoulder and jumped onto the back of the bike. This bike wasn't as flashy as the Ducati—a matte black color, shorter in length and not as shiny.

Kerim looked hot on any motorcycle as far as Cristal was concerned.

Kerim revved the engine and glanced over his left shoulder to check the traffic.

Cristal saw Harry standing on the sidewalk, his shiny blue eyes stabbing her a hundred times with his piercing stare. He shook his head as Kerim pulled out into the street.

ALTHOUGH THERE WAS A BREEZE, the evening air was heavy and her sweat clung to her like a heavy coat. Kerim weaved in and out of the chaotic traffic like a seasoned local. Plumes of black smoke from the tailpipes of cars and trucks as they rode past filled her lungs. She could taste the diesel fuel in her throat. When he turned off onto a side street, she marveled at how many homes could be squeezed onto one street.

She watched rows and rows of short, three-story buildings pass by them; they all seemed to have the same crumbling alabaster, sand-colored stucco with splashes of spray-painted graffiti angrily emblazoned here and there.

Air-conditioning units stuck out from windows and grey satellite dishes pointed their noses in a south-easterly direction. But regardless of the passing terrain, Kerim adeptly swerved around the narrow streets with motorbikes, scooters, and cars half-parked on the sidewalks and on the road.

Teenagers and twenty-something adults hung out around shops and small grocery stores, apparently unmoved by the warm temperatures of the season. She saw soldiers walking by and thought of how safe she should be feeling. But what she couldn't see were all the seniors and families who were tucked into their private residences. Presumably those people were probably trying to cool off with what little relief their window air-conditioners could provide.

As Kerim leaned into a corner, wafts of hashish hit her sense of smell. A loud group of young men were horsing around in an alley lane. From a boom box, a rap-style song played *Shalom Shady*, loudly. It was a wildly popular rap star whose Hebrew/English rap songs played day and night on the TV music video channel and on the radio stations. The boys jumped around, dancing and mimicking the rapper's moves.

Kerim decelerated and turned into a driveway in front of metal grey gates. He stopped the bike for a moment, letting the engine idle.

Cristal heard the sounds of people scrambling and voices calling out, "Kerim is back."

The gates creaked open. Kerim rode inside the cemented lot. Gabriel greeted him and when he saw Cristal, he grinned from ear to ear.

"Hey, Cristal! Glad you finally decided to visit the bachelor pad."

He helped her off the bike, and immediately rambled on about what he and Rinaldo had done earlier in the day.

She watched Kerim disappear into the house. He didn't even bother to wait for her.

"Rinaldo and Raffe are inside. Come in. We just picked up pizza. I'm sure you're starving."

"Yeah, I'm definitely hungry, come to think of it," she managed to say.

She followed Gabriel inside a narrow hallway and up the stairs.

Her eyes adjusted to the dim lighting, as she entered what she guessed was the living room.

The place was cluttered with shoes piled up on the side of the doorway. Tons of family photos adorned the walls, and she laughed when she saw all the books and papers piled up on the coffee table. The only modern treasure in the room was a 52-inch flat screen TV that hung on the wall next to the fireplace.

"Come into the kitchen. That's where everyone is," Gabriel teased while gesturing with his hand for her to follow him.

They walked into the kitchen through another dark hallway that easily was double the size of her hotel room. Rinaldo sat in one corner of the room and he was chatting with a girl while he smoked a water pipe, which was popularly known in the Middle East as *sheesha*. Kerim was deep in conversation with someone and his back was turned to her. She thought it was strange that no one even noticed her when she entered the room.

"Come, the pizza is on the counter. Help yourself. Don't be shy," Gabriel said, waving to the open pizza boxes.

She walked over, her mouth ready to bite into a juicy slice. Her eyes widened when she saw that the pizza was covered with yellow corn niblets.

"Corn?" she asked.

"It's an Israeli specialty," Kerim announced.

She turned and saw Kerim standing behind her. He was half-smiling, not as pissed-off-looking as he was earlier, much to her relief.

"I guess it would be impolite to refuse to eat it?" she asked, smiling.

Kerim looked over his shoulder, and said, "This is Raffe."

Raffe was short, coming only up to Kerim's shoulder. His skin was honey-brown colored and his hair was a pile of black curls crowning the top of his head. He was muscular, dressed in a black T-shirt and ripped blue jeans. He stared at her with eyes so black, they looked like they were filled with liquid ink.

"*Ma nishma*," he said in a deep guttural voice, putting his fist up.

Cristal remembered that this meant *what's up* but she forgot how to respond.

She looked over at Kerim who motioned with his hand for her to raise her fist up. *Oh, yes,* she thought. Kerim had taught her how to greet people with a fist pump.

Raffe smirked as he touched his fist with hers. She felt an electrical shock run through her body. Suddenly, a feeling surged through her that she didn't understand, and everything inside her began to put her on alert.

Raffe shot Kerim a look, grabbed a bottle of beer from the counter and bumped against Cristal slightly as he walked past her out of the room. She thought she heard him say something, but she wasn't sure.

"Don't worry. He's harmless," Kerim said as he put his arm around her.

"He creeps me out," she said. "Who is he?"

Kerim gave her a kiss on her forehead.

Is that his way of shutting me up?

Rinaldo approached both of them and asked, "So, Kerim, were you serious when you said that we're all going to the wall tonight?"

He had an anxious look on his face.

Kerim smirked, lifting his chin, which was his way of saying *yes*.

"Without Harry's approval?" Rinaldo asked.

"We don't need his permission," Kerim said.

Cristal sensed that he was trying to control his temper.

Gabriel joined the circle and voiced his concern, by saying, "It doesn't feel right, Kerim. I mean, Harry is our leader, and he told us that we couldn't go there without him giving us the green light."

Cristal's head began to spin. *What wall? Why did Kerim want to go there? And what was so special about that place?*

"You don't have to come. None of you have to come. But if you want to know the truth, you don't need to wait for Harry to tell us when."

Kerim put his arm around Cristal's shoulder, and he told her, "Come on. Let's go!"

She swallowed hard, acknowledging in her brain what she had to do. Her heart started beating faster. Taking deep breaths, she tried to control her heart rate. She told herself, "*Calm down.*"

"I'm coming with you," Gabriel said. "I always wanted to find out what the big deal was about that place."

Rinaldo's body language was not in agreement with Gabriel.

Rinaldo said, "No way, guys. I 'a' stay here and wait for Harry's call. He has his reasons for saying not to 'a' go without him. I have a big trust for him."

He turned around and went back to the corner where he had left the girl pouting.

"Let's go," Kerim said.

Cristal wanted to say something, but she decided it wasn't the right time. Sometimes keeping quiet is better than asking too many questions.

THEY RODE for over an hour on the motorcycle with Cristal's arms tightly wrapped around Kerim's waist. Gabriel had caught a ride with Kerim's friends in their mini-bus. Cristal had hoped that they would have ridden with them, but she realized that Kerim liked to do things his way.

She closed her eyes for most of the trip, feeling drained of all her energy. Only once did she glance up to see a highway route sign that said 60. *How far is this wall?*

"Don't fall asleep. Don't want you to fall off," Kerim called back to her.

She mumbled, "I feel awful."

He squeezed her arm and encouraged her by saying, "We should be there soon."

She pressed her head tightly into his back, hoping he was right.

"Trust no one," her dad's voice said in her head. *"Today will be the beginning of The End. Stay strong and have faith."*

"No! Stop!" she hollered, shaking her head, and not wanting to hear the voices anymore.

Kerim turned his head towards her and yelled, over the noise of the road, "Are you all right? Do you want me to stop?"

"I wasn't talking to you," she said.

That's when she realized that what she had said sounded crazy.

"I mean, I thought I was going to be sick. But I think I'm okay. We're not that far. Are we?"

She felt his hand on her arm.

"We're almost there. You must be really tired. I can't hear any of your thoughts," he said with a soft chuckle.

Well, that's good to know, she thought to herself.

CHAPTER 19
SAFE ZONE

Zero: video chat in 15 min
Onyx: see you then

Joanna looked over at Jenna who was sitting on the couch, busy typing on her laptop. Although, she had agreed for her to move in temporarily, living with Jenna was driving her crazy.

The sound of the chat tool notification alert interrupted her thoughts. She quickly read the message.

"Was it Harry? What did he say?" Jenna asked raising one eyebrow.

"Yeah, he wants to video chat soon," Joanna said.

"Awesome. Okay, I'm going to set up beside you, so he can't see me."

Jenna stood up, grabbed her laptop, walked over and sat down on the chair beside her.

"Great," Joanna mumbled to herself. *What did I get myself into? Not only do I have the boss interrogating me at work, I've got Jenna bossing me around at home.*

Every day at GN, senior management was breathing down her neck. Joanna knew that if she revealed Harry's breach in security, she would only be revealing her own role. She wasn't ready to be hauled into prison over this.

Jenna turned to her, and asked, "Joanna, why don't you introduce me to Harry?"

"What?" Joanna couldn't believe her ears. "Are you crazy? If he even suspects that I am talking to a non-Truth Seeker, he's going to cut me loose. And where would that get you?"

Jenna bit her lip, a sign that she was thinking up one of her crazy plans.

"No way, Jenna. You just sit quietly right where you are. Or else, I'm going to call this whole thing off," she snapped.

Jenna sighed, and then said, "Okay, okay. Take a pill. I'll sit over here and behave."

Joanna threw her a dirty look but knew that it was pointless. Jenna was so thick-skinned that nothing ever fazed her. She only worried about getting what she was after—no matter what it took.

"You know, I don't know if Kerim Ilgaz changed his name, because I can't find much on him," Jenna said, reaching for her glass and taking a sip.

"Oh?" Joanna frowned.

"He has absolutely no digital tattoo on the internet. No website, no social network. Not even an email account. I asked my contacts in Istanbul to find out more about him. All I could get was that he was in the military for four years. He has no family, no friends, nothing. As far as the database records show, before 2009, he was a ghost."

Joanna said, "Well, maybe he did change his name. If he was in the military, maybe he was a secret agent or something. That would explain why he doesn't have a footprint online. For all we know, he's still under cover."

"You know what, Joanna, I think you are onto something," Jenna said, grinning like a kid who had just been handed an ice cream cone. "I'm going to see if my CIA contacts can find something on him."

"Seriously? You've got CIA contacts?"

She gave her a wry smile.

Jenna shrugged.

"CIA agents are a dime a dozen these days with all the national security measures that President Roshenbaum brought in."

"Funny, I voted for Roshenbaum, thinking he'd protect our rights, but it looks like he's worse than Sanders."

"Yeah, who would guess that General Sanders would be more liberal than Roshenbaum," Jenna replied. "But hey, as long as you instill enough fear in people, they'll all line up and give away their rights like candy."

The sound of the video chat alert interrupted their conversation. Joanna raised her finger to her lips, motioning to Jenna to keep quiet.

Joanna clicked on Harry's avatar and the video chat window opened, filling her screen. He was dressed in an ocean blue short-sleeved button shirt, which was opened at the neckline showing off his golden skin.

Harry looks real good with a tan, she thought to herself. She also noticed that his eyes seemed to reflect the blue from his shirt.

"Onyx, I don't have much time. Do you have the data I asked you for yesterday?"

"Hello to you too, *Zero*," she replied.

"Onyx, I need that data now."

She bit her tongue, trying hard not to glance over at Jenna who was drinking in Harry's every word.

"Sending it now," she said in the most professional tone she could muster.

Harry's eyes looked down until the file was received on his end.

"File received. Good job, Onyx," he said.

She smiled despite herself, her cheeks probably turning all shades of pink. Jenna was going to harass her later, she was sure of it.

"Lionheart knows about the data that we retrieved from the restricted server. She tasked me to find proof that you and Dr. S. breached security."

He scowled, absorbing the news.

"Stick with protocol. Divert *the Lion* away from us by using this data I'm sending now."

She waited until the file downloaded on her computer. "Confirming receipt."

"Also, if Shadow contacts you, flag it with me. Don't reveal any intel to him. Until I have cleared him, consider him a hostile."

She could hear Jenna gasp. Joanna kicked her foot under the table.

"Roger that," Joanna replied.

She knew not to ask questions, but she could feel Jenna growing anxious.

"*Zero*, anything I need to know about Shadow?" she asked.

Harry shook his head, but his face look pained.

"Your next mission. Find out the correlation between these numbers..." he said, while typing in the text window.

Zero: 11132013, 56609, 14350109, 57740910, 17300304

"Where did you get these numbers from?" she asked, but then bit her tongue, realizing afterwards that she shouldn't have asked.

Harry's eyebrows raised slightly. Preparing herself for the lecture, she was surprised when he smiled instead.

"Yes, it would help put things in context if you knew what the source was. We have been gathering reports of people having dreams or visions since the earthquake. These are the numbers that many have reported seeing in their visions," he said quietly.

She smiled to herself. This was the first time Harry had shared crucial intel with her.

"We will get onto this a.s.a.p."

Jenna kicked her under the table. Joanna glanced over to her and realized her mistake before whipping her eyes back to the screen.

Luckily, Harry's eyes were focused on his keyboard as he was typing.

Zero: Evacuate to safe zone ASAP. This is not a drill.

Safe zone? In the Truth Seekers' game, this meant that danger was afoot either from incoming fire or WMDs, or more commonly known as weapons of mass destruction. Harry had shown the team the Safe Zone during orientation training. It was located in a hidden underground bunker, a few blocks from the GN office. Gabriel had made a sarcastic comment saying, "Harry's really taking the online game beyond Virtual Reality."

Onyx: What's going on?
Zero: Follow protocol. Will contact you in 10 hours.

Harry logged off the video chat. She closed the lid of her laptop, her mind still absorbing his orders.

"So, what did he text you?" Jenna asked.

Joanna froze, processing next steps.

"Joanna, are you going to tell me or what?"

When reality finally sunk in, she turned to her and said, "Pack your stuff. We have to get out of here."

"What are you talking about?" Jenna laughed.

Joanna grabbed both her shoulders and shook her hard.

"Did you hear what I said? Get your crap, now!"

Jenna's eyes widened, her tanned skin turning visibly pale.

"What's going on, Joanna? You're scaring me."

The confident Jenna Adams looked like she was going to wet her pants.

Joanna said in a low, soft voice, "If you want to live, we have to leave now."

CHAPTER 20
THIS IS NOT RIGHT

THE TIMING WAS ALL WRONG. He couldn't believe Cristal would run off with Kerim, someone she barely knew. He wished he could have told her the truth. The truth about the tests that Dr. Saeed had been secretly performing on her while she was "working" at GN. She didn't realize that the computer monitor she was using had a special sensor connected to the camera, which monitored her brain activity and breathing. Nor did she know that the mouse had tiny needles that pricked her finger and collected micro-samples of her blood.

Harry slammed his fist on the table.

"I told those guys not to go to the black hole locations with Cristal."

Not one of them understood how dangerous this would be. The rules were clear, just like in the Truth Seekers' game; no one was allowed to question him about the missions.

But this wasn't the game anymore, and Harry didn't know what to do. He had to figure out which location they were heading to. There were three black hole locations—one was in Eilat, the most southern part of Israel; one was in the West Bank near Bethlehem in the central part; and one closest to the GN office in Akko in the northern part.

If only he could pick up the GPS tracking signal from Cristal's cell phone. He had spent the last five minutes trying to search for it on the computer terminal in the GN's IT office, with no luck. *And where in the hell was Dr. Saeed?* He walked out of the room and down the hallway to the medical lab. It was late in the evening and only staff with security clearance could work after hours. Fortunately, Harry happened to be one of them.

Two Israeli security guards armed with rifles walked by him. He looked them straight in the eye and nodded his head. They looked down at his GN staff ID around his neck before walking past him.

Harry began analyzing which location would be the most possible out of the three black hole locations Kerim would be headed to. He hoped that it was the one in Akko, the closest to the GN office. It made the most sense for them to go there, given that he had told Kerim and Rinaldo to stay away from that specific location. But if he were wrong, he would be going in the completely opposite direction of the other black hole locations, which meant losing precious time. He needed time to stop Cristal from reaching the black hole.

He turned down the hallway to the medical labs until he reached the one that GN had assigned to Dr. Saeed. The room looked empty through the glass window in the door. He decided to go inside anyway and check.

He swiped his keycard and opened the door. It was dark inside the room. It took a few minutes before his eyes could adjust to the darkness. No sign of Dr. Saeed. He was about to turn around and leave, concluding that he would have to go find Cristal and Kerim without him.

He paused and listened. He swore he could hear muffled voices. He looked across the room and noticed light streaming from under the closet door on the far wall. Cautiously, he walked towards the light. The sound of two male voices in a deep conversation was becoming louder.

When he reached the door, he noticed it was slightly ajar. He peeked into the crack and saw that the back of the closet was a fake wall with a door half hidden by boxes. He remembered going into the closet many times to get supplies, but he had never noticed the door before. Now it seemed that the hidden door was open, and the light was coming from behind it—*a secret room?*

He pushed the door open enough so that he could slide into the closet. The voices were audible now. He recognized one as being Dr. Saeed's.

"You're going to jeopardize everything. Don't do this," Dr. Saeed was saying.

"All the experiments have proven our theories are correct. The girl is the key to unlocking the power that I need."

That male voice sounded familiar. Harry's heart started pounding hard against his chest. His hands suddenly felt clammy. He took a step closer to see inside. He was surprised that behind the hidden door was a high-tech medical laboratory with expensive medical equipment, machines, and computers. His eyes panned to where Dr. Saeed was standing, close to an examining table, his back facing him.

Harry saw the shape of the man Dr. Saeed was talking to. The color of his pants was tan, and the sleeve of his shirt, beige. Dr. Saeed moved slightly to the left, giving him a full view of the man he was speaking to. Harry sucked in his breath.

"I don't know what to say. You show up here and want everyone to believe that you just arrived today?" Dr. Saeed shook his head. "We buried you, for crying out loud."

PART III
IF YOU ONLY KNEW

The dawn has come
    And the morning sun's rays
    Streak the painted sky, warm crimson shades of orchard rose
    While the ocean tide caresses the damp dark beach
    And a silent tear slides down her cheek.
    AR Vasquez

CHAPTER 21
IN THE FLESH

"SAEED, I'M TELLING YOU, it worked! I'm living proof."

Harry watched in shock as Aaron Doub danced around in a circle, shaking his arms like a mad man.

This man is not my father. My father is dead. This stranger has my father's voice, his face, and even his ridiculous comb-over that hides his bald spot. Aaron Doub looked exactly the same way he did the last time Harry saw him alive.

Dr. Saeed said in a soft voice, "But you were declared dead at the hospital."

The hair on Harry's arms stood on end. What is going on here?

"Don't say that word! You know I don't like that word."

That was the kind of eccentric talk Harry knew and grew up with —the paranoid scientist. *My father is alive.* Somehow the shock didn't register, as it should have. Aaron's presence made a strange kind of sense in Harry's mind.

"Sorry, Aaron. I forgot," Dr. Saeed said quietly. "My only guess is that something must have happened at the hospital. If someone took you from the hospital and then cremated another body, then that could explain how we were made to believe that you died."

"Saeed! Didn't I tell you NOT to use that word?"

He jumped up and down like an infuriated gorilla.

"Would you like me to give you a sedative? It looks like the trip has made you quite anxious," Dr. Saeed said, crossing his arms.

"No! No sedative," Aaron said, his anger suddenly dissipating. He slumped down on the examination bed, and whispered, in a breathy tone, "I don't feel well."

"You've just travelled through time at superluminal speeds. The human body travelling at warp drive, theoretically speaking, could affect the atomic molecular structure of the person, agitating the body at a cellular level. You need to hydrate and rest. When you are rested, I will do some testing."

Dr. Saeed helped Aaron step down off the examination table and got him safely situated on a nearby bed. He reached for a folded sheet and covered Aaron's body.

"Here, drink this," Dr. Saeed said, as he handed Aaron a plastic cup filled with water.

"Straw, please?" Aaron asked, his eyes looking up at Dr. Saeed.

He grasped the sheet, pulled it up to his neck, and waited while Dr. Saeed put a straw into the cup.

"Thank you, Saeed. I don't know what I'd do without you," he said, grinning sheepishly.

"Now, now, Aaron. Just relax. I need you to tell me everything you can remember before you arrived here," Dr. Saeed said in a soothing tone.

Harry could barely contain his desire to burst into the room and demand answers from Dr. Saeed and his father. Fortunately, the Truth Seeker in him knew enough to stay still. He had to watch and listen.

What other information has Dr. Saeed withheld from me?

Tasting the same bitter betrayal Cristal must have felt towards him, he knew this was karma—*what goes around does come around*.

Dr. Saeed turned away for a moment, his back to Harry. When he turned around, he was holding a needle syringe. He gently pulled up Aaron's sleeve, wiped his arm with a cotton swab, and injected what Harry assumed was a mild sedative.

Aaron smiled as his body relaxed.

"Ah, you always knew how to make me feel better, Saeed."

Dr. Saeed pulled a chair up beside the bed and sat down.

"Okay, are you ready to tell me everything?"

Aaron closed his eyes in affirmation. Harry was baffled. He never remembered seeing his dad like this before—vulnerable and almost childlike.

Harry looked at his watch. Time was ticking by. If he didn't leave soon, Cristal would reach the black hole, and—the thought of what could happen made his gut wrench. Torn and emotionally sucker-punched, Harry was reluctant to leave. The truth he sought might have been a complete lie. Dr. Saeed and Aaron were both in on something, and now, Harry's world was turned completely upside down. He knew that whatever secrets those two shared would definitely affect every Truth Seeker, not just himself.

"Do you remember the dinner party at your house?" Dr. Saeed asked in a monotone voice, hypnotically soothing.

Aaron mumbled to himself, his eyes still closed.

"Ah, yes. I was telling everyone about our latest findings. About time travel."

He chuckled quietly, grasping the top of the sheet tightly.

"Go on..." Dr. Saeed prompted him.

"I don't remember the rest of the dinner. I must have fallen asleep. I woke up and found myself in a lab, just like this. Yes, yes...I remember now. There were people around me wearing hospital masks. I tried to say something, but I couldn't."

"Do you remember what they were saying?" Dr. Saeed asked.

"Nothing. No one was talking. I thought that was strange. I tried to get up, but I couldn't move a muscle. Then they all left the room, leaving me alone on the gurney. That's when I felt the room shaking. My body started convulsing violently. I felt the air being squeezed from my lungs. I wasn't scared though," he said, half whispering.

"Why weren't you scared?"

"It almost felt like the first time when we almost succeeded. I felt myself slipping out of reality. The atoms in my body were pulling apart; the room was spinning around me. And then there was a flash of white light. Then blackness, like I was falling into a deep endless pit."

Dr. Saeed frowned, nodding his head as if he was picturing what Aaron was saying in his mind.

"It seemed like I would fall forever, horrified and worried that it would never stop. After what seemed an eternity, I felt all my atoms rush together like a magnetic wave pulling all my cells towards the core of my body."

Harry was puzzled by Aaron's words. *What was he talking about?*

"And then I felt as if a bus had hit me. I thought I was going to die. Then I was stumbling in here," Aaron said, his eyes opening.

He looked around.

"Looks like you have upgraded a lot of things, since I've been here."

He's been here before? What the --?

"Like I said, it has been five years. Harry and I were trying to continue the work that you started. But this lab, I've kept secret. I don't want GN sticking their noses into our work. I also wanted to protect Harry."

"Ahhh, Harry. How is my boy?" Aaron asked, smiling.

"He's not a boy, anymore. He's a man now with a doctorate. A true genius. Just like you said he'd be," Dr. Saeed replied.

"Yes, we succeeded in proving my theory. Inducing the chemical changes in the cells of a genius—one whose soul is pure of mortal sin. That was the secret to it all."

I can't believe you both used me.

Dr. Saeed stood up and leaned over the bed.

"But that doesn't explain how you time travelled here."

Aaron's voice melted into a nostalgic lilt.

"You're right. We did try altering the general chemical composition of my nucleic acids. Nothing seemed to come of it, except for my sudden hair loss."

Dr. Saeed chuckled.

"That wasn't sudden, Aaron. It's just that you hadn't seen the top of your head in a really long time."

Aaron scowled and turned away.

Dr. Saeed seemed to ignore him.

"In order to time travel, you had to be near the vicinity of a black hole, and there had to be enough power or energy to enable you to transport to here—the future."

Aaron rolled his eyes, saying, "I told you, the energy was coming from inside that room. It seemed that those masked persons turned on the energy when they left the room."

"Similar to an X-ray technician going into a booth before powering up the machine on a patient," Dr. Saeed said.

Despite marveling at the idea that such a machine capable of time travel existed, Harry was seething with anger. He and his mother had trusted Dr. Saeed. But he was just using them both like lab rats. Suddenly, he could hear Cristal's voice in his head saying those same words to him not too long ago.

His mother's journal had mentioned how much she trusted Dr. Saeed, because he had helped prescribe the medication she needed to cope with the loss of her husband. He had driven her to the GN psychiatric visits. But now, Harry doubted Dr. Saeed's intentions. Harry didn't know what his mother, Bina, had said to her psychiatrist, but he was certain that she never told anyone about her secret journal.

"And Bina? Is she safe? Did you manage to test our theory on her?"

"Bina is fine. She finally got over your death," he started to say, but he paused and corrected himself. "She finally got over her loss of you. The tests I conducted on her were a success, just as we had hoped for."

Tests? On my mother? Did he kidnap her?

The phone in his pocket began vibrating, followed by the text notification alert. *Crap.* He fumbled to turn it off.

He glanced up to see Dr. Saeed frown and tilt his head. He stood up and started walking towards the closet. His face had a deathly calm expression, as if he was about to capture his prey.

I've never seen him look like this before.

What was more odd was the fact that his eyes seemed to be glowing a fluorescent shade of yellow. Harry wasn't sure if the shadows in the closet were playing tricks with his mind, but he wasn't going to wait to find out.

"Harry? Is that you?"

Harry shook his head in confusion. He acknowledged in his brain that it was the voice of Dr. Saeed, and yet it wasn't. The tone was much deeper with a reverberation that sounded like nails scratching across a blackboard.

Now, I know I'm not imagining things.

He stumbled backwards, bumping into the boxes of supplies behind him. Quickly regaining his balance, he turned and ran out of the closet and back into the lab. He had to get the hell out of there.

He ran to the doors, flinging them open. Behind him, he swore he could hear a weird "wooshing" sound.

Holy crap. Don't look back.

He sprinted down the hallway, rushing past the security guards. They both called out for him to stop. *No f'ing way!*

He made it into the stairwell, picking up the pace as he sped like a bullet down two flights of stairs to the bottom floor where he reached the emergency exit doors. Power reading a sign written in Hebrew that was pasted on one door, "Alarmed. In case of fire, push to open," he slammed his body against the handles, shoving the doors open.

The clanging of the alarms rang into the air.

He bolted towards the parking lot. *What the heck am I running from?*

The rational side of his brain told him he was being paranoid. But his natural instincts told him to run even faster.

He reached the parking lot and saw that his car was one of only three left in the lot. He ran towards it, ripped open the driver-side door, and jumped in, slamming the door behind him. He jabbed the button to lock the doors while he shoved his foot on the brakes and pushed the button to start the engine.

Why I am so frigging terrified? It's just Dr. Saeed, for crying out loud.

Out of desperation he called out, "Mom, if you can hear me, please help."

He couldn't believe that he would resort to calling out for his missing mother. He must be losing it.

Check your phone. The answer is there.

"Mom?"

He whipped his head around. He was certain that the sound of her voice was coming from the back seat of the car. But his anticipation was replaced with a sad disappointment. No one was there.

"Freak, I must be hallucinating."

Hurry, Harry, there isn't much time.

He spun around again. No one else was in the car. *I must be going nuts.* Why is my mind playing tricks on me?

Something inside him made him pause and reach for his phone. When he swiped the screen to unlock his phone, he saw that he had a text message waiting for him.

He wondered if his mother was trying to communicate with him. Text message received.

Graphix: Update: We picked up *Lioness* from airport. *Mist* and *Shadow* are here in Akko. Sending you video of Shadow talking to Raffe. Looks intense but u need to translate. Awaiting your orders.

There was no time to psychoanalyze the situation. He shoved the gear stick into the Drive position and pressed the gas pedal to the floor.

In the distance, the sound of the sirens from the fire trucks was approaching fast. He breathed a sigh of relief. *Whatever was after him, if there was anything, was gone.*

Hearing a "wooshing" noise again behind his head, he glanced into his rearview mirror to see what it was. His heart started pounding fast and hard; fear surged through his veins.

Something was staring back at him in the mirror—it resembled Dr. Saeed's face, but from the yellow glow in its eyes, Harry was definitely sure it wasn't human.

CHAPTER 22
AKKO

T HE SALTY KISS OF THE balmy sea breeze caressed Cristal's cheeks while the evening sun was setting on the horizon, producing a fiery orange emblem against an angry red sky.

Will we ever see blue skies again? She wondered to herself. Since the earthquake, the sky remained a shade of red. Some countries reported a blood-red color, while others described the sky as being red with pockets of blue peeking through the orange and white clouds.

Experts claimed it was simply due to the refraction of light related to the sun's position and the scattering of electromagnetic radiation through the atmosphere. Basically, it was mankind's fault for using the Earth as its toilet.

Global Nation, founders of the group, "A Sustainable Planet," blamed the red color on global warming caused by environmental pollution destroying the Earth's ozone layer.

Scientists countered this theory proving global warming could not be the cause, due to the fact that the planet was becoming colder, not warmer. If the scientists were correct, then what was really causing the sky to turn red? Deep down inside, she feared that she was the cause of it.

Kerim and Cristal sat on a four-foot high wall of sandstone blocks, which stretched for miles along the shoreline. Over the wall was a steep drop to the crashing waves of the Mediterranean Sea below.

Her senses were captivated by everything around her. The breeze from the water tickled her skin while the vibrant smells filled her nose with a combination of scents—salt from the sea, seaweed, kelp entwining their leaves across the seabed, and families of fish inhabiting the warm water.

When they had first arrived in Akko, Kerim had seemed edgier than usual.

"Can't believe I forgot my smokes," he had mumbled over and over as they walked down the streets of the ancient town looking for a shop that sold Lucky Strike, the only brand of cigarettes he smoked.

Despite being an anti-smoker herself, the fact that Kerim was a smoker never bothered her. It seemed to be a natural part of his makeup.

She glanced over at Kerim, and it looked as if he was deep in thought. The scene reminded her of Apollo, the Greek god—handsome, confident, and strong.

"Are you feeling better?" he asked quietly, taking one last drag from his cigarette before tossing it on the ground.

"What's taking Gabriel so long?" she asked.

"He probably stopped to get something to eat. I heard Rinaldo saying he wanted to grab a baguette."

"I see..." she said, and looked off into the distance.

How do I tell him about what happened at the hotel?

"I know what you're thinking," Kerim said softly.

"You do?" *Are you reading my thoughts again?*

He gave her a smug grin.

"Yeah, actually, I could hear you the whole time. I didn't realize that I resembled a Greek god."

Cristal felt her cheeks grow hot with embarrassment.

She took a breath to regain her composure, and said, "The lady from the plane, the one you switched seats with, she's a National Security Agent."

Kerim's eyebrow rose up slightly. "You mean Ms. Full-Bodied Mama? You're joking."

She shook her head, and answered, "No, she's for real. She showed us some photos she had taken while you were sleeping on the plane."

Kerim clenched his hand, and then said, "And?"

"There was this weird glow around your head in all the photos," she said quietly. "And she also had a video clip to prove to Harry that it wasn't a Photoshop job."

"Wow, and you both believed that crap?" he asked.

"It looked very real."

Kerim wrapped his arms around her and pulled her towards him. She enjoyed the embrace.

Why did she feel so safe in his arms?

"Let's say that this is true," he began. "What do you think this light around my head could be?"

She stared deeply into his eyes. "Yaffa called it a halo."

"Ah, Yaffa," he mumbled. "She called it a halo."

He repeated the words as if trying to understand the full meaning behind them.

"It did look like a halo, Kerim. But I also took a photo of you. Remember? You were doing the peace sign and there was no halo around you."

"Victory sign," he interrupted.

She rolled her eyes. "Yes, victory sign. My point is, when I took the photo of you, there was no light around your head. I don't know how to explain why there was a light in Yaffa's photos."

"It's the music," he murmured to himself.

"What did you say?" Cristal asked.

"When you and I were listening to the music, we were connected to each other in our minds. I could read your thoughts and you could read mine. It's possible maybe that with the human eye, the light is not visible. But on digital photos, this light is visible."

Cristal shook her head, trying to process what Kerim had just said. "I don't know. That sounds pretty far-fetched."

Kerim looked at her then, his eyes probing into hers.

"Isn't everything that happened after the earthquake, as you say, 'far-fetched?' Like the fact we can communicate without words, and how about you seeing Harry's mother's image in the sky on the day of the earthquake? Isn't that far-fetched? Something is happening with us. With the world."

She was about to say something, ready to argue his points, but instead, she fell silent. He was right. Right about everything.

He continued talking to her while his fingers gently stroked her arms, waking the hidden passion inside her.

"I've been having strange dreams and visions lately. And my headaches seem to be getting worse. I feel like my brain is trying to tell me that there is something I'm supposed to do. But I can't remember what it is."

She still didn't know what to think or what to say.

"Do you know that being here could be dangerous?" he asked her quietly.

His expression of concern was unnerving, but his caresses were numbing the anxiety in her mind.

"Because of what happened in New York?" she asked.

"We're going to enter one of the black holes," he said, very matter-of-factly as he stared straight into her eyes. "We don't know what will happen. You do know that Harry didn't want us to bring you, don't you?"

"If that's the case, why did you?"

Kerim reached into his leather jacket and took out his smart phone. "I want you to see something."

He swiped the phone's surface, tapped a few buttons, and handed the phone to her.

On the screen, there was a photo of what looked like an open journal with handwritten notes.

She glanced over at him, and asked, "What is this?"

He tipped his chin up slightly. It was his way of telling her to go check it out. She had hung around him long enough by now to understand the subtle meaning behind his mannerisms and gestures.

She swiped the screen to zoom in on the photo until the words were legible.

The dreams are coming all the time now. They used to scare me but now I welcome them. I am able to remember in detail the last one. The numbers keep repeating in my brain. 11132013, 56609, 14350109, 57740910, 17300304.

I'm writing this before sleep steals me back into the darkness of my nightmares.

The darkness enclosed around me, like it always did in my dreams. I was wandering the streets of an old city surrounded by walls that towered high above. Everything seemed familiar to me...the sights, the sounds the smells. The air was filled with a salty mugginess. Behind the walls, must be the sea, I thought as I stumbled down the street. I wanted to go towards the water but I could hear voices ahead of me. For some unexplainable reason, I felt drawn towards the sound.

By the wall, there was a young couple. The woman was remarkably pretty; the man, dark and mysterious. Their voices sounded concerned but I couldn't make out the words. I inched closer, wondering why I was here and why I was seeing this.

Suddenly, someone grabbed me. I turned to see who it was but saw nothing. I tried to break free, to scream for help but I was paralyzed. I watched as a dark cloud descended onto the woman. It had tentacle-like arms wrapping around her, strangling and choking her. The man was trying to pull her free but he was no match for this thing. I could see the woman's eyes wide with fright. The tentacles were literally squeezing the life out of her right before my eyes. It was then that the man lifted his arms and looked up to the heavens crying out in a language that sounded like Latin. A brilliant white light exploded across the sky. The earth began upheaving beneath my feet. I struggled to move and realized that I had been freed. I turned to run, to save my cowardly self.

But I could see the woman was also freed from the arms of the dark cloud. She was screaming, or seemed to be. I could not hear over the thunderous roar. I could see why she was overwrought. The man was being torn apart by the rays of the white light that had snaked its way down from the sky. I saw him explode into a white light, a transparent being. It was then that he rose up, as if a force were pulling him. He reached out to the woman, she reaching out to him. But their hands never touched. He was pulled away, almost violently, like a rag doll, up into the sky.

And then I awoke.

Bina Schwartz

CHAPTER 23

'48

CRISTAL LOOKED UP FROM the phone, meeting Kerim's gaze.

"Where did you get a hold of the journal?" she managed to say.

Her mind was reeling, her brain still trying to process the information.

"I broke into Harry's office this morning and found it in a hidden safe under his desk," he said.

She handed the phone back to him. "Was this all that was in it?"

"No, there's a lot more."

"I noticed the numbers. I thought they looked familiar. They are the same ones Harry asked us to find out what the correlation between them were."

"And?" He raised one eyebrow.

"He never told us what the numbers were or where they came from. So we thought they were secret codes and we tried to break them. But now, it is so obvious."

She couldn't believe how simple it was.

Kerim was watching, waiting for her to continue.

"11132013, 56609, 14350109, 57740910, 17300304. It's a date, not a code. It's today's date formatted by the different calendars—Gregorian, Julian, Islamic, Hebrew, Coptic."

His eyes widened.

"Today's date? November 13, 2013. Did Harry know?"

She shook her head, giving him a wry smile. "I don't think so. One weakness about Harry, once he's got his mind focused on something, he gets stuck on that theory for a long time until he figures out that there are other options. He makes the simplest things so complicated sometimes."

They fell into an awkward silence—both of them avoiding the real discussion they should be having. What Bina had written could have been a premonition about what was about to happen. Cristal trembled at the thought.

Kerim reached out and pulled her towards him. "Cristal, I don't want to lose you," he said, his voice thick with emotion. "But it seems that time is running out."

"No," she said, pulling away. "Don't say that. Nothing's going to happen. We're all going to be okay. I don't want to think too far ahead. Let's just enjoy the moment we have right now."

Hot tears burned her cheeks, but she refused to brush them away.

Kerim reached up and held her face, kissing her cheeks. He gently wiped the tears from her eyes.

"Okay, okay. Let's stop talking about this."

She was relieved that he had closed the topic.

"Come on, smile for me. You know I hate to see you cry," he whispered.

She gave him a small smile—happy to be in his arms, to be in love, and to be loved back.

The sound of a blaring car horn interrupted her thoughts. Cristal glanced at the street and saw a silver-grey minivan pulling into an empty space behind Kerim's motorcycle.

"Kerim, Cristal, let's go!"

Gabriel hollered at them as he stuck his head out of the passenger window, his arm waving frantically for them to come.

Kerim waved his hand back at him. "Come on," he said to her, placing his arm around her shoulder.

She laced hers around his waist. A part of her was worried that Kerim was right about the fact that time was running out. Stubbornly, she pushed the thought far back in her mind.

Everything is going to be okay. Dear God, help us.

A group of young men who had been sitting on a bench nearby was now standing around the van. There were four of them—one large guy in a blue T-shirt and black jeans, two of medium build in polo shirts and blue jeans, and the last one was the smallest in a white shirt and black pants. They seemed to be glaring at Kerim warily.

Cristal felt Kerim's hand tighten around her shoulder.

"Don't worry," he said in a hushed tone.

He let go of her shoulder and walked cautiously towards the men.

"Marhaba," he said.

She knew this meant *hello* in Arabic.

"Ah-layne," the large one responded, which was a way to say hello or welcome.

Kerim continued talking in Arabic with them. She could see Gabriel getting out of the van to join them. The conversation sounded tense, their body language strained.

Although she hated politics, Cristal had been tracking the news about President Roshenbaum's involvement with the Israeli and Palestinian peace talks. The State of Palestine would finally become a reality at the end of the month when the peace agreement was signed. That was good news for Palestinians in the West Bank and Gaza; not so good news for the Israeli-Arab population, sometimes referred to as "the Arabs of `48." These were the Palestinians who, as Wikipedia described, were the Palestinians "standing fast, not fleeing during the War of 1948, unlike those who left and became refugees in neighboring countries."

Now, generations later, the "Arabs of '48" and their children had become Israeli citizens. Facing racism as a minority population within Israel while at the same time considered traitors by Arab countries and other Palestinians outside of Israel, "the Arabs of '48" could not embrace their own identity as Palestinians or as Israelis. To the outside world, they were neither Palestinian nor Jew.

Now with the peace talks, rumors that right wing government parties were going to pass a law to force Israeli-Arabs to transfer to the State of Palestine, thereby losing their Israeli citizenship brought uneasiness between Israeli-Arabs and Israeli-Jews. Although Cristal hated the politics of it all, she understood their uneasiness. As an American-Mexican, the idea of being forced to transfer to Mexico and then stripping her American citizenship was incomprehensible.

The back door of the van on the passenger's side opened, and Rinaldo stepped out onto the street. He was followed by a smaller person. When she squinted her eyes, she recognized who it was. Serena.

Why was she here? Harry probably sent for her without telling me.

Rinaldo walked towards the larger man, motioning to Gabriel with his head, who moved behind the other three.

The larger man looked over his shoulder at Rinaldo before saying something to Kerim.

From the driver side of the van, the door opened and Raffe came out. The look of annoyance on his face was intimidating; revealing a fury she sensed was larger than the situation at hand.

He advanced towards them in confident strides causing the young men to step back.

Raffe spoke to them, and his Arabic sounded rougher than Kerim's and the young men, probably due to his Hebrew accent. They spoke back and forth for a few minutes.

Cristal held her breath, wondering what the conversation was about. Kerim came up alongside Raffe, and they both continued speaking to the four of them.

The large man suddenly cracked a smile. He turned to the others whose grave expressions thawed into playful grins.

Kerim looked over his shoulder at her and signaled with his eyes for her to come to him. He gave her the thumbs up, letting her know that everything was fine.

She walked over and stood beside him.

"Hello, nice lady," the larger one said with a grin.

"Hello," she said.

Kerim reached over and squeezed her hand reassuringly.

"I study Engleesh in Canada. My name is Walid," he said, his smile growing wider. "You like Akko? It is very, very, old city."

"I'm Cristal. Yes, it is very beautiful."

From the corner of her eye, she noticed that Rinaldo and Gabriel were having a side conversation of their own, whispering to each other.

What was going on?

She shifted her focus back.

Walid announced, "I see you before."

Cristal's eyes widened. "Me? No, I don't think so."

Walid took a step closer, unable to hide his excitement. "Yes, yes...it is you. The day the big earthquake, it happen in Megiddo. My town. I see you in my dream."

Kerim's hand tightened over hers. "It's okay, Cristal. Remember. Nothing is far-fetched."

She gulped. Walid was waving his arm like an excited fan asking a famous celebrity for an autograph.

"I do not forget you. You very pretty. I not forget." He turned around and translated what he said to his friends.

Kerim said, "It's time to go." He turned to Walid and said something in Arabic.

Walid said, "Tammam. Y'alla!"

She knew this meant, *Okay, let's go.*

He waved to the others to follow him as he walked towards the red VW Golf hatchback that was parked in the space in front of Kerim's motorcycle.

Kerim glanced over, and said, "We're going to the wall."

"We?" she asked.

He grabbed her hand and led her to the motorcycle.

"Yeah, Walid and his friends are coming with us."

CHAPTER 24
MIND GAMES

HARRY WAS DRIVING FAST. Way too fast.

"Slow down," said the voice that could pass as Dr. Saeed's.

Harry glanced at the rearview mirror. Dr. Saeed lounged in the back seat, on the passenger side. No crazy eyes, no spinning head. He was just normal.

Considering the circumstances, Harry should have been somewhat relieved. Earlier, he had imagined vampire teeth sinking into the back of his neck. Thank God, that didn't happen.

He heard his mother's voice say, *"Barukh atah Adonai Eloheinu melekh ha'olam, ha'motzi lehem min ha-aretz."* Blessed are You, Lord, our God, King of the Universe, Who brings forth bread from the earth.

It was the only prayer his mother taught him in Hebrew. She made him say it before every meal, despite Aaron's forbidding any forms of religious expression in their home.

Saying the prayer was meaningless to Harry. Just some words he would mumble before taking a mouthful of his dinner. If it made his mother happy, he wasn't going to argue with her. Why he could hear his mother saying the prayer now was just another mystery to him.

Focus on finding out more about the monster in the back of my car.

"Dr. Saeed, or is that your real name? Are you going to tell me what you are?" he asked, trying to keep his voice steady.

"You're talking very strangely, Harry," Dr. Saeed replied. "Are you okay?" he said, again in that soothing voice of his.

His hands gripped the wheel.

Okay, play the game. Buy some time.

"I don't know, Dr. Saeed. I guess I'm not quite myself," he said.

"Ah, yes. You must have fallen asleep when you were waiting for me in the car."

Fallen asleep?

"I don't know what you're talking about," he said. "As far as I recall, I was in my car by myself, ready to drive away from GN. And then you showed up from nowhere in the back seat."

"Harry, now it's my turn to say, 'I don't know what you're talking about.' Don't you remember calling me? You said to meet you at your car and that it was urgent. That we had to go find Cristal before she ended up at one of the black hole locations."

Flashes of memory exploded into Harry's head.

He could see himself leaning his head back on the headrest, the seat slightly reclined. There was a knock on the glass. He opened his eyes and saw Dr. Saeed. He unlocked the door to let Dr. Saeed in.

Harry swerved the car, almost clipping a truck beside him.

The driver waved his hand out the window and yelled, "*Mh ath hvshh shath 'evshh?*" What do you think you're doing?

"Get a hold of yourself," Dr. Saeed said. "Do you want me to drive?"

Harry felt disoriented, unsure of himself. Did he, in fact, dream up the whole thing? The secret lab? Seeing his dad? Dr. Saeed's yellow eyes? He did recall having trouble sleeping the last few nights. Was he suffering from sleep deprivation?

"I said, do you want me to drive?"

Harry glanced over his shoulder. Dr. Saeed was looking at him with concern. He had to admit that he did not look like a crazy monster. If it was all a dream, then he didn't have to be afraid of him.

"Why?" Harry asked, hoping to sound lighthearted. "You don't like my Israeli style of driving?"

Dr. Saeed chuckled softly. "Glad to see you are feeling better. Your choice of words always amuses me."

Wait a minute, Harry thought. *Why was Dr. Saeed in the back seat? He never rides in the back seat.*

Harry took a deep breath. "You comfortable back there, Dr. Saeed?" He looked up in the mirror to see a smile curl up on the Doc's face.

"Yes, Harry. Thanks for forcing me to sit back here. You know I prefer to ride shot gun."

*Okay, good answer. Maybe I **am** losing my mind. Play it cool.*

"You know I had a vision today," Harry said quietly.

"Oh? We have some time before we get there. Care to tell me what it was?"

Harry saw the exit sign to Akko coming up on the right. They were about twenty minutes away from the black hole.

"I saw Aaron. He time travelled here to GN," Harry said quietly.

He looked over his right shoulder to check the blind spot before changing lanes. He caught Dr. Saeed's eye in the mirror.

It twitched, I'm sure of it.

Harry's mind was reeling as he tried to contemplate why Dr. Saeed, or more like Mr. Hyde, was playing ignorant. A thought crossed his mind.

Maybe he didn't know that his cover was blown.

"And what if that were true?" Dr. Saeed asked, as if luring him in, in his usual reserved way. "How would you feel about that?"

"Ah, come on. Don't talk to me like you're my shrink."

"You do realize we both don't know what will happen when we

arrive at the black hole. It could be the end of us all." Dr. Saeed paused. "So, humor an old friend, Harry."

As Harry drove into the city of Akko, he had to slow down as he approached a roundabout. The Israeli Transportation Department installed the roundabouts to control the speed of drivers. However, it only encouraged the locals to speed around them like Indy race car drivers on crack cocaine. His mother always told him to "do as the locals do," so he slammed his foot on the gas and whipped around the roundabout, hurtling Dr. Saeed against the side door, and then toppling him over to the opposite door as Harry gunned the car into a sharp right.

Dr. Saeed never wore a seatbelt stating that, "If it is my time to leave this timeline, then so be it. I want to enjoy the ride; not feel strapped in like a prisoner."

"Dr. Saeed, you okay back there?" Harry asked, chuckling to himself.

Dr. Saeed grabbed the back of his chair in an attempt to balance himself. "Harry, that isn't funny," he snapped.

In the rearview mirror, Harry saw that he had pulled himself up. He began fixing his shirt and patting the sides of his hair flat.

What a self-centered prick.

They sat in an uncomfortable silence while he drove them through the old city. Harry noticed that there were a lot of cars on the road with mostly guys not much younger than him, out for a joy ride, heading towards the beach—to hang out or kill time.

Speaking of time, Harry realized that he should use this opportunity to squeeze more intel out of Dr. Saeed.

He cleared his throat before saying, "Aaron is here. I can feel it. Call me crazy, but in my vision, Aaron told me that he travelled through time to get here."

"He told you this?" Dr. Saeed leaned his head forward between the front seats, causing Harry to almost jump out of his skin.

"Freak! Do you want to get us killed?" he cried out, as he swerved inches away from sideswiping a parked car.

"Oh, sorry," Dr. Saeed said as he leaned back. "It's just that your vision was not a dream, Harry."

Harry could hear the excitement in his voice. Is he for real? So Dr. Saeed really didn't have a clue that Harry knew his secrets. If the good doctor was attempting to make him doubt himself, it wasn't working. Deep down in his gut, Harry knew he saw something not from this world.

He realized that he must be developing a sixth sense, like Cristal. And why would he be surprised? Aaron and Dr. Saeed admitted they had been experimenting on him, too. Deception had a bitter taste. Aaron admitted having tested on himself, too. And who was to say that Dr. Saeed wasn't one of Aaron's volunteer test subjects?

"Harry, are you listening? Your father is alive."

"Yes, I know," Harry replied calmly. "You and I both know that he time travelled here." He looked up at the mirror to see his reaction.

Dr. Saeed's eyes met his gaze. "No, he didn't. Although he would want everyone to believe that."

Harry swerved the car over to the side of the road, putting the stick shift into park. He spun around.

Screw logic. He wanted answers.

"What the heck are you talking about? Stop talking in circles!"

Dr. Saeed stared at him, looking almost contrite. He said, "He didn't die five years ago."

Harry was completely baffled at what he was hearing. He had expected Dr. Saeed to explain how his father went FTL, or faster than light speed, on warp drive while time travelling here from the past to the present.

"Sorry, I don't get it. What are you trying to say?"

Dr. Saeed took a deep breath, getting ready to tell him in his "once upon a time" way.

Harry groaned. "Skip the long explanations and just tell me the Cliff notes' version."

Dr. Saeed replied, "Yes, of course. The data that the Truth Seekers' team has been decoding uncovered something that GN has been hiding."

Harry sighed. "Cut to the chase, Dr. Saeed. You're killing me over here."

Dr. Saeed cleared his throat and wiped the sweat from his brow.

Man, he's either a great actor or he's got something really good to tell me.

"Okay, in short, GN faked your father's death. That was the big secret that GN had encrypted on their secure servers."

What in the...?

"Are you talking about the data Cristal and Joanna were decoding? We knew that it was a huge secret they were hiding. But you're telling me the secret was that they had faked Aaron's death?"

Dr. Saeed said, "No, no. It's more than that. But I'm still trying to figure it out. And could you please refer to him as your father? He is your father, after all."

"Okay, so you're saying Aaron was in on it?" Harry said, putting emphasis on the name *Aaron* as he spat out the words.

"No, definitely not. They kept your father in a drug-induced coma. For what reason, I'm not sure."

He took a deep breath. "The decrypted data Joanna provided had been running through your software program before you left to see Cristal. The data revealed that there was a secret room at GN. I went in search for this room and found that it was guarded. Fortunately, I was able to convince the guards that I had clearance. I found your father in the secret lab."

Harry pounced on this bit of information. "Secret lab?"

"Yes, yes! GN has a secret lab."

"Where was it?" he asked with a sneer in his voice.

Dr. Saeed wasn't admitting he had a secret lab behind the hidden door in the closet of his lab.

"In the South wing basement," Dr. Saeed continued. "When I found him in a comatose state, I administered Zolpidem into his IV drip. He woke up an hour later, although he was quite incoherent at first. I managed to get him dressed and walk him out of the secret lab back to my lab."

What a backstabbing, lying sack of sh*t! He played me all along for an idiot, a dumb kid moron. And to think I believed him and put Cristal and all the Truth Seekers in freaking danger.

Son of a b*tch. He'd be damned if Dr. Saeed used him and Cristal as pawns ever again. Harry was about to say something when the car started to shake slightly. His head felt woozy as he turned to face forward—trying to steady himself. Seconds later, a thunderous sound roared in the sky above them.

"Dear God," Harry muttered.

Dr. Saeed grabbed his shoulder. "Drive, Harry. We must get to the black hole before anything happens!"

The earth shook subtly beneath the car in waves. Harry shifted gears and pressed his foot down on the gas.

CHAPTER 25
THE WALL

WHEN THE FIRST tremors on the ground started, Kerim and Cristal were standing in front of the walls of the old fortress of Akko, which loomed sixty feet high above them. Seconds later, Raffe appeared out of nowhere. Something about this guy unhinged her nerves. However, now was not the time to pinpoint exactly what it was.

Cristal clung to Kerim as the ground gently swayed back and forth—the swaying reminded her of when she was standing in her stepfather's boat while it was docked in the marina. Not that he knew how to drive the thing. He only used it to throw cocktail parties for his wealthy dental clients and show off his perfect family.

As suddenly as the shaking began, it stopped. Kerim looked down at her, almost the way he looked at Gabriel, right after the earthquake in New York with his "Are you serious?" face.

She released her arms around him and mumbled, "Sorry, not sure what got into me."

Walid and two of his friends were standing off to the side, a few feet from her. Where were the rest of the Truth Seekers?

"Mizz Cristal," Walid called out as he ran up to her. "Did you feel the shake of the ground?"

Cristal glanced over at Kerim who had moved over to the van. He was quietly talking with Raffe, a grim expression on his face. She noticed that he was shaking his head, several times in fact. Cristal didn't want to even surmise what they were saying to each other.

She turned back to Walid who was wide-eyed and nervous, obviously aware of the imminent danger, despite appearing to be calm. He smiled at her in a reassuring way.

"Do not be scared," he said. "Allah is here and if it is His will, then we must trust Him."

She knew "Allah" meant "God," and she didn't think this was the time or place to suddenly become religious.

"You believe in God, yes?" he asked.

"Of course, I do," she said. "I'm just not religious. What I mean is, I don't go to church or anything like that."

He said, "You need not go to a place to talk to God. He is here. Everywhere."

He raised his hands up to the sky to emphasize his point.

"Yes, you're right," she said, happy to hear he wasn't going to try to preach to her.

That was one of her biggest pet peeves. Born in a Roman Catholic family, her mother always tried to shove her beliefs down her throat. The more she did this, the more she wanted to run away from her.

Her senses picked up something in the air. The ground under her right foot shifted ever so slightly while her ears were picking up a high-pitched sound, similar to what she had heard before the earthquake in New York.

Oh, no, not again.

Her heart began beating faster, her lungs starting to burn.

"Calm down. You can control this," her father's voice whispered in her ear.

She frantically looked over at Kerim, but he was still in a deep discussion with Raffe.

"Mizz Cristal?"

She turned back to Walid whose eyes were deep with concern.

"I'm sorry, Walid," she finally managed to say. "I'm not feeling very well."

He turned and said something to his friend who dashed over to the car. Shortly after, he ran back with a bottle of water in his hand, stopping, and holding it out to her.

"For me?" she asked.

He smiled shyly, his eyes looking down at his feet.

Cristal was overwhelmed with Walid and the boy's sweet kindness. Her heart filled with warmth and gratitude. She took the water bottle gratefully, and smiled back.

"Thank you very much. It is very kind of you," she said.

The young man looked up at her briefly, his face turning red. Walid patted him on the back, signaling for him to step back.

"Drink. It is good to drink," Walid said to her, motioning with his hands.

She smiled, removed the cap from the bottle, and tilted it to her lips. The cold water spilled into her mouth, quenching her thirst, relaxing her breathing, and decreasing her pulse rate.

When she looked up, she gave Walid a warm smile. "You were right. The water has made me feel ten times better already."

Now it was his turn to blush. "Very happy to help you, Mizz Cristal."

She was about to respond when his smile quickly left his face, his eyebrows furrowed into a knot; he stared at the bottle in her hand.

She glanced down, too, wondering what he was looking at. The water was bubbling out of the bottle, like someone opening a bottle of pop after shaking it.

"Cristal?"

She looked up and saw Gabriel standing in front of her, a worried look crossing his face. Rinaldo and Serena were behind him, with similar stunned expressions on their faces.

"Drop the bottle, Cristal! It might have been poisoned!" Serena cried out. She ran up to Walid and twisted his arm behind his back.

Cristal dropped the bottle to the ground, spilling the water, or whatever it was, onto the street.

"That is a lie!" Walid yelled. "Let me go!"

She was certain Walid was not trying to kill her. Although she had no way to prove this, her sixth sense assured her that he had nothing but respect for her.

Her confidence in herself began to waver, when suddenly everything around her started fading in and out.

Had someone really put poison in the bottle?

She saw Kerim running towards her and Raffe was grabbing his arm, trying to hold him back.

Several flashes of bright white light streaked across the sky, followed by cracks of thunder. The thunder clapped in back-to-back succession as if someone up there was massively pissed off and lighting gargantuan firecrackers.

To celebrate the impending storm?

Did she really think that? She shook her head wondering why her mind wasn't making much sense. Another boom from the sky. And another and another. The sounds were so deafening, and they triggered car alarms to go off in the street.

"Kerim!" she cried out, or tried to.

She couldn't hear herself above the thunderous roar.

Out of the corner of her eye, she saw a small silver car drive up onto the sidewalk. It was gunning towards Kerim before skidding to a stop beside him. A young man jumped out of the car and ran toward her.

Harry?

"Cristal!" Harry screamed, but his voice was covered by the roaring thunder.

When he opened his mouth, she could only hear the thunder as if it were rumbling out from his lips.

She felt the ground swaying beneath her feet.

Oh, God, I think I'm going to be sick, she thought to herself. She could not stop herself from falling over. Help me, she thought, while trying to form the words to speak, but couldn't.

A strong arm grabbed her by the waist, keeping her steady. Then she felt someone else hold onto her other arm. Cristal glanced down and saw Kerim holding onto her waist. Dr. Saeed was on the other side of her, holding her arm.

How did Dr. Saeed get here? Did he ride here with Harry?

Harry was running towards her, his eyes wide with fright, his mouth open, screaming words that she could not understand over the thunderous booming sound above them.

"Just relax, Cristal," Dr. Saeed said in his usual reassuring tone, his voice cutting through the noise like a sharp knife slicing a stick of butter. "Let me take you to the car."

No, no, no!

She pushed Dr. Saeed away from her, and leaned her full weight on Kerim. The ground churned violently beneath her feet.

"I'm here, Cristal. Don't be scared," Kerim said into her ear. He lifted her into his arms, carrying her away.

She knew he would do whatever it took to get her to a safe place. She saw a flash of light and then heard more claps of thunder. She noticed the ground was rippling in small waves. Another lurch of the ground sent Kerim forward releasing her from his arms.

In her delirium, Cristal felt herself flying into the air, in slow motion, in a free-fall upward.

Free-fall upward?

It sounded ridiculous, but it was true. Higher and higher she felt herself ascending. Over her shoulder, the fortress wall behind her was whipping down the higher she rose.

She glanced down and saw Harry, frantic, screaming. He was

waving his hands above his head. Gabriel and Rinaldo seemed to be holding onto Kerim for dear life. And little Serena, she seemed so lost standing there by herself, staring up at her.

Cristal blinked her eyes, still not fully comprehending what was happening. She realized she was floating ten feet, now twenty feet above all of them.

How is this happening?

Glancing down, she watched a grey cloud-like shape rise up from the ground, almost like a mini tornado, twisting and growing. It was rising off the ground and forming into a shape. Before she could blink her eyes, the grey cloud transformed into an eagle, and its wings spanned the length of the van. The eagle flapped its glorious wings and flew up into the sky, circling and soaring between the lightning strikes and swirling black clouds. It gracefully ascended higher, until it hovered in front of her.

She stared in amazement when the eagle transformed once again. Everything, except for the wings, metamorphosed into the shape of a man—his body was like a translucent silvery glow. She squinted at his face, which was taking shape now with a nose, eyes, and mouth.

I recognize this face, she thought to herself.

Gasping, she realized that this being that was levitating in front of her, seemingly oblivious to the demented storm around them, was none other than Kerim's strange friend, Raffe.

Raffe's lips twitched into a smile, as if acknowledging her findings.

"Who are you?" she tried to ask, but the wind swallowed her words.

No time for that! Take my hand! His voice bellowed out in her head, and the pain cut through her like sharp knives.

Her body began convulsing; her head felt like it was going to explode.

Raffe reached his hand out and touched her forehead. As soon as she felt his hand on her, the pain was replaced with a sweet relief.

His voice entered her mind again.

Sorry, I haven't taken this form for many years. I have forgotten how sensitive you humans are. I will decrease the volume of my thoughts so as not to mutate your brain cells.

"Are you serious?" she asked, half hoping that she had passed out and this was just some preposterous hallucination. A thought came to her mind. How come when she first met him, he didn't speak any English?

He opened his mouth to speak, and said, "The English language is so rudimentary. I prefer not to speak it unless necessary. I shall speak to you with my mouth instead of my thoughts, as this requires less energy. Best to conserve my energy for later."

He sounded like a foreign exchange student learning English. His words came out in a staccato-like fashion. He spoke with proper grammar, but he lacked the idioms and slang terms that most native speakers use.

He continued, "As I said earlier, there is no time. Give me your hand, now. You must do this willingly."

Despite the terrifying situation she was in, the fact that she was suspended fifty feet up in the air didn't prevent her natural stubbornness from surfacing.

Glowering at him with defiance in her eyes, she asked "Or what?"

His nostrils flared slightly before he said, "Or the demon that is pinning you to the wall will drop you to your death below. But the frightening part will not be the fall. That part is fairly quick and simple. Really, the ghastly part would be the way "it" would manipulate you to release your soul willingly before you crash to the ground."

Oh, my God.

The fear that would wake her up in her sleep, the dreams, visions, voices in her head, all started flooding back to her.

"Ah, yes. Calling out to our Lord our God, Father to all, is a good start," Raffe said in his monotone voice.

He reached out his hand. "Do you believe in God?" he asked bluntly.

"Yes, of course I do. I have always had a strong faith in God. But I definitely don't believe in religion."

Now, why did she have to admit that?

Raffe shrugged.

"Religion is a manmade institution. Not made by the Almighty One. So, no worries. You have passed the test."

He motioned to her with his hand to come towards him.

"That's it?" she asked.

Suddenly, she felt as if something released her, causing her to free-fall again, but this time, it was downward and much, much faster—dizzyingly faster. She reached out her hand, or tried to.

"Dear God, help me! I don't want to die!" she screamed in her head.

When she realized that her body was about to go "splat" onto the ground below, she felt arms underneath her swooping her up, and holding her tight. Her body felt like it was drifting down like a feather falling from the sky. She realized Raffe had caught her and was flying her down into the arms of Kerim.

The bile was rising in her throat against her will. The disorientation in her head and general chaos around her was overwhelming. The many faces looking down at her revealed their mouths moving, but their words were unintelligible. The storm still blustered above. All this made her want to crawl up into a fetal position and retreat.

She watched Raffe transform from a winged angel back into his human form. Then she noticed that the storm seemed to have lost its anger, and the thunder was now a dull roar.

"Cristal, are you okay?"

She turned and saw Kerim's face looking down on her. His look of sincere concern comforted her. But, before she could enjoy the moment, another voice interrupted her thoughts.

"Cristal, oh, my God!"

She turned and saw Harry. His eyes were as wide as saucers, and terror was written all over his face.

"Please, be okay. I don't know what I'd do without you."

Tears were streaking down his cheeks.

Harry Doubt, crying for me? I must be tripping out.

Kerim pulled her closer to himself and away from Harry. She let her head lean against his chest, and felt calmed when listening to his heartbeat.

"Let's lie you down in the van," he said, as he carried her away from the gawkers.

A loud sound like a firecracker blasting in her ear made him freeze in his tracks. She saw Kerim staring at something in front of him. With the little bit of energy she had left, she turned to see what it was.

Oh, freak. This can't be happening!

CHAPTER 26
NOT SO LUCKY

STANDING A FEW FEET AWAY, Yaffa Bauer had her 9mm semiautomatic pistol pointed at Kerim's chest. Cristal saw several other agents in black suits surrounding her, and they had their weapons drawn.

"Kerim Ilgaz," she said, "I am Yaffa Bauer, National Security Agent, informing you that you are suspected of terrorist activity against the State of Israel and the world. You do not have to say anything. Whatever you say might be used as evidence against you. Refraining from answering questions might strengthen the evidence against you. Place the woman down and come with us without resistance."

Kerim stood as still as a statue.

Yaffa said something to the other agents and they instantly came swarming around them. She saw Raffe, in human form, walking up to Yaffa, who waved her gun at him, yelling and screaming that she was about to shoot.

He spoke to her in Hebrew, saying something that caused her to stop. She motioned to the other agents to stand down.

Turning to Kerim, she said, "Okay, your friend here is going to prove that you are not behind these terrorist activities. I've asked my men to stand down. I will be going with you. But if you try anything, I will have my men shoot you on the spot."

Kerim stared at Raffe, unsure of his plans.

Kerim, did you know that Raffe was this weird bird man? She spoke to Kerim in her thoughts.

He frowned, his jawline tensing. That meant no.

Yaffa turned, faced them and asked, "Who wants to join us to find out the truth?"

Walid looked over his shoulder at his friends, who seemed to be shrinking in their shoes, before stepping forward. "I will join."

Harry stepped forward, and said, "I'm in!"

"Count me in," Serena said.

Rinaldo replied, "If they go, I go."

Harry said, "Leave Cristal here. She needs to rest."

Yaffa shook her head firmly. "No, she is necessary."

She pointed at Gabriel, and said, "He must come, too."

Gabriel looked around and pointed at himself, saying, "Who, me?" He turned to Kerim, his eyebrows arched.

Yaffa nodded. "We watch you every day. You and Kerim are conspirators."

Gabriel said, "No, not me. I'm just a gamer. I'm not a terrorist."

Kerim shot him a glare, his nostrils flaring. He whispered in Cristal's ear, "Can you stand?"

She said, "Yes, I'm feeling better now."

He gently lowered Cristal to the ground, and then offered his hand for her to grab, helping her stand.

He reached up and held her face in his hands, searching deep into her eyes. "Cristal, do you believe in kismet? A pre-destined moment, where fate steers your life? In a direction you never meant to go. Where reality takes a back seat to what only your heart appears to know?"

Her heart filled with a warmness she had always yearned to feel. She had never heard such beautiful words before.

"Kerim, that sounds like a poem. It's so beautiful."

He smiled, his grey eyes softening. She could see tiny tears sparkling in the corners.

He said, "It's a song I wrote for you. When we get out of here, I promise I'll sing it to you."

She swallowed hard, tears welling in her eyes. "Why does it sound like you're saying goodbye?" There was an ache in her heart, and the pain felt like it was being twisted like a dagger.

He kissed the tip of his finger and then placed it on her lips.

"Believe in me and never doubt. Promise?"

She gulped, unable to say anything. Hot tears streamed down her face.

Why does this feel like you're leaving me? I can't live without you.

"Promise me," he whispered, his eyes were probing hers while his fingers stroked the tears away.

Finally, she agreed and said, "I promise."

"Very touching. For an innocent man, you bleat like a martyr. Let's get moving," Yaffa called out.

Kerim gave Yaffa a dirty look. With his fists clenched, he took a step forward. Cristal could feel her heart racing.

Don't do anything crazy, Kerim!

Yaffa raised her gun and pointed it at him. "Don't move, or I'll shoot."

The other agents followed suit and leveled their weapons.

"Cristal is staying here," Kerim said in a low voice. He reached out his hand and guided Cristal towards Raffe.

The agents raised their guns.

"Kerim!" Cristal cried out as she stumbled into Raffe's arms.

She frantically looked over at Serena and Rinaldo, praying that they could do something, anything to stop this. Counting the number of agents that surrounded them, along with where they were positioned, and the weapons directly pointed at them, she realized that they were outnumbered and couldn't win this battle.

Not surprisingly, it was Harry who stepped forward.

"Kerim, let's just all go together," he said.

He placed his hand on Kerim's shoulder.

"We will prove that you and Gabriel are innocent. And we can deal with Yaffa later."

Kerim gave him a blank stare, his body tensing. He shoved Harry's arm off his shoulder.

"Leave me alone," he said. Reaching for his Lucky Strikes, he mumbled, "I need a smoke."

Yaffa's face tensed and squared off.

Cristal's mouth dropped open.

Oh, sh*t! She thinks it's a gun!

"Yaffa! Stop! It's just a pack of cigarettes!" Cristal cried out. She tried to run, but Raffe wouldn't let her go.

Gabriel saw Yaffa's reaction and rushed towards Kerim, shoving him out of the way.

Shots rang out. Bap! Bap! Bap!

In horror, Cristal watched Gabriel crumple to the ground as the bullets pierced his body. Kerim and Harry grabbed him before his head hit the pavement.

"Gabriel!" Their screams echoed in the air.

"Raffe, I demand you to let me go!" Cristal cried out.

Raffe blinked and released her arm. He stepped back and let her pass. With a burst of adrenalin, she sprinted towards Gabriel's motionless body. Serena and Harry knelt beside him, trying to revive him.

She flung herself down on the ground, kneeling into the pool of blood that was pouring out from underneath his back. She scanned his body to see where the exit wounds were and saw three bullet holes in his chest. The voice of her CPR coach rang in her head.

Focus, Cristal. Remember the ABC's of CPR. Check Airways, Breathing, and Circulation.

Her training in cardiopulmonary resuscitation was keeping her calm. No air, no breath, but there was a shallow pulse.

Good. He's still alive. Hang in there, Gabriel.

She blew into his mouth and pumped his chest.

Breathe, darnit, breathe.

After thirty compressions, he still wasn't breathing. The weak beat of his pulse earlier had kept her hopes up, but to her shock, there was no more pulse. Serena knelt down beside her grabbing Gabriel's wrist.

"Keep going, Cristal," she said.

Cristal began pounding on his ribs in desperation.

Beat! Come on, beat for me!

She slammed her fist into his chest over and over. Serena shook her head to indicate that there was still no pulse.

"Gabriel! Don't! Don't die on me!" Cristal said.

After a few minutes, she realized it was too late. Her body was shaking, and her energy spent.

"Cristal, he's gone," she heard Serena say quietly.

"Nooooo!" she screamed, with her eyes looking up into the dark purple sky. "How could You take him?"

Like a mad woman, with hands that were soaked in Gabriel's blood, she shook her fists at the heavens. She demanded an answer from a silent God.

"Cristal, please don't," Harry said, his voice broken with anguish.

He wrapped his arms around her as she moaned into his shoulder. Suddenly her body shivered and she felt herself sobbing from delirium. She opened her eyes and saw Walid and the others standing around watching her.

Cristal pushed Harry's arms away and stood up, numb with grief.

Where was Kerim?

She looked over and saw a group of agents standing next to their vehicles. The sight of those bottom-feeding sharks made her heart pound so hard in her chest that she felt like her ribs were going to crack.

"Cristal!" Kerim called out.

She turned and saw him being held by two agents, while waiting for another agent to open the door to the vehicle.

"Kerim!" She called out, running towards him.

Yaffa stepped into her path with her hand extended out, signaling for her to stop.

"Stay back, girl. You don't want to be arrested, too," Yaffa said with a sneer.

"Murderer!" Cristal screamed, as she felt every cell in her body begging to snap Yaffa's neck.

She imagined all the ways she could destroy her when a bolt of energy from inside her body blasted out from her hands shoving Yaffa on top of another agent.

Cristal stared at her hands in amazement.

Holy crap, did I do that?

Cristal bolted over to Kerim and threw her arms around him. The two agents released him, their eyes wide with fright. They stepped back without question.

"You can't leave. You can't," she said, sobbing into his shoulder.

Kerim kissed her on the cheek, saying, "Cristal, please stop crying. It rips me apart to see you like this."

The fury was burning inside of her.

Keep calm, she told herself.

All of a sudden, a high-pitched sound blasted through the air. The ground began shifting in violent waves, ripping cement and uprooting trees. Kerim reached down and grabbed her around the waist and began running.

The fear she felt earlier was replaced with an incredible calm, her perspective morphing into a third party observer watching the chaos unfold. Everyone around was scattering and looking for cover.

Serena and Rinaldo ran to the van; the agents scrambled to a building across the street. Walid's friends crouched beside the wall.

Harry stood motionless, staring at her with a sad look on his face. He was no longer her protector.

"Stop or I'll shoot!"

Now what?

Cristal turned and found herself looking into the barrel of Yaffa's gun.

CHAPTER 27
BEGINNING OF THE END

THE GROUND BENEATH THE agent's feet rose and fell, but Yaffa looked determined to ride the waves like a skilled surfer.

"You are no longer grounded. Gabriel is gone. You've unleashed your powers. The powers you have are beyond what you can imagine. You must trust yourself," her father's voice said in her head.

"I said stop this or I will shoot!" Yaffa's words came out like a shrill cry.

A gunshot filled the air. She felt the bullet whip past her ear.

An incredible force shoved Cristal, throwing her body twenty feet into the wall. She bounced off and landed on the ground bruising her shoulder. The rest of her seemed relatively unharmed. She pushed herself up to find herself eye to eye with Dr. Saeed.

"Dr. Saeed?" she asked. She heard a crash as giant chunks of the wall came down around them.

"Cristal!" Kerim and Harry were racing to her, dodging pieces of the falling wall and jumping over the ground-swelling waves.

When she turned, Raffe was standing beside her, facing Dr. Saeed.

"Leave her alone," Raffe growled.

"Come with me, Cristal," Dr. Saeed said, motioning to her.

"No, Cristal! Don't listen to him!" Harry screamed.

The ground shifted violently, causing Dr. Saeed to fall backwards.

"Dr. Saeed!" Cristal cried.

She tried running towards him, but her legs wouldn't budge. They were planted to the ground, the energy shooting through her body up into the sky.

Dr. Saeed stood up, trying to steady himself when Harry tackled him, sending him back onto the ground. They wrestled as the ground rippled around them.

Dr. Saeed flung Harry, thrusting him up in the air like a sack of potatoes before slamming him into the wall. In the blink of an eye, Dr. Saeed bounced up from the ground effortlessly. His body rotated in a fluid-like motion, and he began running, although it looked more like flying, towards Cristal.

She realized then it wasn't Dr. Saeed, although it resembled him in appearance. This thing's eyes were glowing an odd neon yellow color; its body was transparent, and its mouth opened revealing a row of two-inch long fangs.

What in the world?

She tried to lift her legs to run, but the magnetic energy from the earth held her down.

Dear God!

As if to answer her prayer, a gust of wind brushed past her. Raffe had transformed back into the winged being and was flying towards Dr. Saeed at a speed faster than a shuttle preparing for liftoff.

"I command you to stop," Raffe's voice bellowed.

The vibrations from his words caused more tremors in the ground.

"You can't use that cheap parlor trick on me," the dark spirit said in a voice that sounded almost robotic, deep and guttural with a hollow screeching echo in the tone.

All of a sudden, the dark demon spirit whipped out a black tail about six feet in length and lashed at Raffe's head. Raffe reeled backwards, hurt by the blow.

So he isn't invincible after all, she thought to herself.

Raffe quickly regained his balance, stretched out his wings, and reached behind for something. To her amazement, he drew out a sword—a sword she never imagined existed. The shaft was emblazoned with ornate symbols emblazoned; the blade forged out of pure white energy was the length of Raffe's wing with rays of light gleaming from the edges. Holding the sword forward, Raffe hurtled towards the demon, plunging the blade deep into its chest.

A howl came out of the demon's mouth, a horrific sound not from this world—a terrifying shriek that made the hairs on Cristal's arm stand on end.

The demon spirit morphed back into Dr. Saeed's human physical body and plummeted to the ground. As the human body of Dr. Saeed lay motionless on the ground, she watched a dark shadow rise from it, twisting and writhing in agony.

Raffe waved his sword up in the air, not showing any mercy. The dark shadow demon shrunk back in fear, before turning and slithering down into a large jagged crack on the sidewalk.

The ground expanded and upheaved, before sending fierce tremors in all directions, north, south, east, and west. The great wall behind her was now a mountain of dust.

Harry appeared in front of her, his face pale as a white sheet.

"Cristal," he said. "Kerim isn't who you think he is. You have to believe me. You can't trust him."

"Stop it, Harry," she said, overwhelmed and exhausted with what she had just witnessed.

Harry took a step closer to her, his blue eyes clouded with shadows.

"Listen to me. I just watched this video that Gabriel sent me before he died. He took it when he was still in the van. It's Raffe and Kerim discussing how they were going to eliminate you."

"I said, stop it! Nothing you say is going to change how I feel about Kerim."

"Then, I won't talk," he said as he shoved his phone to her. "Here, watch for yourself."

On the screen was a video of Raffe and Kerim. They were having a deep discussion outside the van. The video must have been taken before she had been lifted up to the tops of the fortress walls, because she could see herself in the background talking with Walid.

Raffe was speaking, but it was in Hebrew, so she couldn't understand a word.

"What does this prove? So they're talking," she snapped at him. "You know I can't understand what they're saying."

This is unreal! Trapped in a pillar of uncontrollable energy and having this ridiculous conversation with Harry.

"If you want to help, figure out how to make me stop this!" she yelled, pointing at the light blasting from her body.

Didn't he care that she was standing here emitting energy like a nuclear power station gone wild?

The force inside her was funnelling up to the heavens from the top of her head and down to the bowels of the earth from the bottoms of her feet.

Where are you, Kerim?

Harry stepped to the side and she saw Raffe, who had metamorphosed back in human form, with Kerim standing beside Dr. Saeed's body. Raffe was waving his arms and yelling in Hebrew, while Kerim was shouting back at him. Suddenly, Dr. Saeed's body sat upright. He was looking around as if he was in a daze.

Okay? Now, what's going on?

Raffe raised his arm with a clenched fist, as if ready to pulverize Dr. Saeed until Kerim's hand caught his arm.

"The demon left the body. You can't hurt the human," she heard Kerim say.

Raffe sneered. "He signed his life away to the devil when he wanted to find the secrets of immortality. This pathetic piece of feces doesn't deserve to live."

Abruptly, Harry turned to her and asked, "Wait a minute, do you understand what they're saying?"

"Of course, I do," she said.

After the words left her mouth, she realized that Kerim and Raffe were speaking in Hebrew.

"I don't get it. How come I can understand them?" she asked Harry.

Harry came closer, his body inches from hers. He grabbed her hand and held it tight. "I don't know either, but I think maybe you always were able to learn languages quickly. You just didn't know how to tap into that part of your brain."

"Seriously? It can't be that simple."

Harry swiped his phone and turned it back to her. "Oh yeah? Watch the video and see for yourself. I bet that you understand what they're saying now," he said.

"You know, I could say you're crazy but after all that's happened today, anything is possible," she replied. "My father spoke to me in my thoughts. He said that Gabriel's death unleashed my hidden powers."

"Your father said that? You know what, that makes absolute sense! Gabriel must have been like a ground wire in an electrical outlet. Before he died, he somehow prevented you from accessing your powers," he said.

"Or, he helped contain the energy from going out of control, like what's happening right now." She pointed to the beam of light blasting through her body.

Harry held his phone up to Cristal. "Are you ready to watch now?" he asked.

Cristal took a deep breath and said, "Yeah, show it to me."

The video started playing from the beginning. It sounded like Raffe was lecturing Kerim.

"Do you remember now? You were sent here to stop her. Not to fall in love with her. When you were changed into human form, we archived your memories and implanted fabricated memories into your human brain. This is the only way our kind can successfully infiltrate humans."

Holy crap! What is he talking about? Cristal thought to herself.

Kerim began speaking. "I am remembering now. The Almighty sent me to stop the dark spirits from entering our spiritual realm," Kerim said.

He speaks so strangely, she thought. *It doesn't sound at all like the way he talks to me. But maybe it's just how my mind is translating this. It's like I'm a Hebrew as a Second Language student and my brain is processing what they're saying too literally.*

Raffe cracked a weird smile, relieved to hear that Kerim was finally coming around. "Kerim, you are one of our greatest warriors. You took on this mission to protect the Kingdom of the Almighty."

Kerim stared off into the distance and said, "And the black holes are the entrances to the secret portals from our world to this world. Only our kind is permitted to travel back and forth. Although, we are able to transport humans to Limbo, Purgatory, or Paradise."

The way he spoke was as if he was repeating something he had learned during his training.

Raffe smiled, and said, "Very good. You are remembering now. Don't worry; it will all come back to you. Your human brain is much too small to fully grasp all of it. Today, you will be transformed back to your natural state, but you must complete your mission. You must eliminate the girl. She is the key to opening the portals for the humans and the demons. Her natural power and abilities are threatening the security of all worlds."

Kerim raised his hand in defiance. "No! I cannot do this! She is an innocent. She has done nothing wrong."

Raffe's expression changed, as if repulsed by Kerim's reaction. "Not only must you do this. You will do this lest you face the wrath of the Almighty."

Is this "angel-speak" or is this how they say things in Hebrew? Do angels really speak like this?

Kerim put his face in his hands. His body was visibly shaking. "I cannot complete this mission. I love her, with every part of my being."

Cristal felt her heart swell despite learning about Kerim's true identity.

He was sent here to kill me?

She was beginning to fully comprehend the meaning of the phrase "Love is blind."

Raffe put his arm around Kerim's shoulders, speaking in a softer tone. "When I first was sent down here, for my first mission, I, too, fell for the charms of the female human persuasion."

Kerim glanced up, and asked, "You did?"

Raffe nodded. "In fact, that is why the Almighty sent me here to make sure you complete your mission. I was sent to destroy Liora Henandez, a Sephardi—a Jew of Spanish ancestry. The Henandez bloodline that goes back centuries is known to have special powers and abilities. He appointed guardian angels to watch over them. Since they were a good people, the guardians were instructed not to harm them but to report if the security of our worlds is breached. For centuries, the Henandez family kept their powers concealed from anyone outside the family. They followed the Almighty's rules and never once did He have to send an archangel for an extraction mission."

Kerim was completely absorbed, listening intently.

"Unfortunately, during the 1960s in this world, it was a time when the humans were rebelling against their parents' beliefs and searching for spiritual independence. Liora was a good woman. Her brother was killed in a war that she believed was senseless. She wanted to fight against injustice, so she joined a group of activists who at the time were uncovering secret experiments without knowing that the scientists were in fact demon possessed humans."

Kerim interrupted, raising his hand. "I remember this. These were the 'Isolating the Soul' experiments. It caused a stir with the Seven Senior Archangels. I didn't understand the significance at the time and why we were put on high alert. Demons are always searching for more effective ways to relinquish humans from their souls with their permission. When I finished my intensive training to become an archangel, I realized how devious demons really were. Instead of threatening humans to give away their souls, they had found a much easier way. They simply asked humans to be test subjects and made them sign release forms thereby giving away their rights to their soul."

Raffe picked up where Kerim left off. "It was not just that. You may have not been briefed, as this is classified information. However, I share this with you as I have been given some leeway by the Almighty to provide you information on a 'need to know' basis. It seems to me this is the time you 'need to know.' The leaders of the dark spirits have always wanted to enter Limbo and Purgatory to steal the souls of those who are waiting to enter the gates of Paradise. If they breach this world and enter ours, this act alone will cause an imbalance between all the worlds, which could lead to catastrophic destruction for the world here and the spirit world. This would thrust good and evil of man and spirit into a war that will end all wars."

Kerim arched his eyebrow. "And what happened with Liora?"

Raffe shrugged as if trying to make the memory seem trivial. "Well, I fell in love with her. It was hard not to. She was beautiful, generous, and had the purest heart I have ever seen in a human. Like you, my memory had been archived, and implanted memories made me believe I was human. It was with Liora that I felt the emotion of love for the first time. Unless we are in pure human form, our kind does not have the capacity of feeling this emotion. When it came time to eliminate her, I was blinded by the love I felt for her. Love is an emotion that you will not forget, but over time, the memories will fade."

Kerim's eyes widened. Cristal realized at the same moment that it was Raffe and Liora that Bina Schwartz saw in her dream.

Kerim asked quietly, "And the Almighty pulled you out of the mission and returned you to Him?"

Raffe's face grew dark as he spoke. "He removed me from the human world and stripped me of my rank. The Almighty demoted me from being a general to a lowly Purgatory Guide. The other archangels scoffed at me. But after getting to know the humans in Purgatory and understanding their suffering and pain, I realized why we have to protect them. Eventually, I was returned to my brigade and given the rank of Admiral."

Kerim smiled wistfully. "I am a colonel in your brigade, Admiral Raphael," he said with a deep respect in his voice. "You mentored me, I remember. But you still haven't told me what happened to Liora."

Raffe replied with a sigh, "The Almighty sent another angel to finish the mission. Once the angel took her from this world, her soul entered the Kingdom. She sits among those who are in the good graces of Him. Here in the human world, she left behind a daughter who was raised by Liora's sister as her own child. She changed her name to 'HERNANDEZ' to protect the child's identity and emigrated from here to Mexico. When the child became an adult, she immigrated to the United States. Don't you see? Cristal Hernandez is Liora's great granddaughter."

SHE SHOOK her head in disbelief. "Harry, this is too much. I'm part of a bloodline that has special powers?" There was no time to think about this now.

She looked up and saw Raffe and Kerim still arguing with each other, oblivious of anything else around them. Maybe that was a good thing. It gave her time to think of what to do next.

Buildings were collapsing; people were getting injured, maybe even dying.

I have to stop this.

"Harry, I'm going to try to close the portal," she said.

"Wait! I have to go through it." Harry grabbed her shoulders. "I believe my mother and your father are there on the other side, in Limbo or whatever Raffe and Kerim were talking about."

He looked at her with determination in his eyes.

"Yes, they have been trying to communicate with us. I think they are alive. I know they are alive."

"I will do my best to bring them back," he said, touching her face.

"I know you will, Harry," she said, as tears slid down her cheeks. She bit her lip. Now was not the time to cry. "Hurry, before they see you," she said. "I will close the portal after you enter. I will make sure Raffe and Kerim won't follow you."

His eyes were dark with concern. "Take care of yourself, okay?"

"Yeah, you know I always do." She smirked and looked into his eyes. "Hurry up before I zap you with my super-duper energy blast."

He smiled. It was just like old times. "I'll be back soon."

Then he stepped to the side of her, into the light and was gone.

Good luck, Harry.

She closed her eyes, concentrating all her thoughts towards the waves of energy that were blasting out from inside of her.

Summoning all the power inside her, she roared, "*I command you to stop!*"

Her eyes opened and the white light that had been rushing

through her had stopped. She checked her feet by taking a step forward and realized she was free. No time to celebrate. She had to get out of there before Raffe "the Bird man" started coming after her.

She ran up to the edge of the sea wall and looked down at the crashing waves below. Glancing back, she saw that she had caught Raffe and Kerim's attention.

I better jump before Raffe stabs me with his light sabre.

Cristal faced the water, closed her eyes and leaped over the edge.

Her body plunged towards the water. She was falling fast. In her mind, she wondered if this was the smartest thing she could have done. She pointed her feet down, anticipating impact. Although she was relatively calm, a part of her was calculating what the chances were of smashing her body against a big rock.

Dumb move.

Before she hit the water, she heard a "woosh" and felt arms underneath her catching her from the fall. Her eyes opened to see it was Kerim holding her tight. His gaze was fixed ahead of him as he carried her upwards. She turned her head and saw, to her amazement, behind his back were glorious silver feathered wings soaring in flight. She checked to see if Kerim's body had become transparent. Thankfully, she could still see his T-shirt and leather jacket. He was in human form, except for the wings.

She wanted to say something but wasn't sure exactly what.

He glanced down briefly and said, "Do not be afraid, Cristal. You have no need to doubt me."

Before she could react, a thunderous voice boomed across the sky making her cringe in fear.

"Complete your mission!" the Voice commanded.

She could feel Kerim's body shudder.

Is he going to drop me?

He whispered to her, "I will put you down, but you must hide. You have the power to do this. Just focus and concentrate. You don't need a black hole to enter the other realm. You can transport back and forth like me."

"I can?" Her jaw dropped.

"You can. Just like you realized today that you have the power to understand many languages. You must believe in yourself."

Kerim made a nosedive to the ground. She held on tightly to his arms.

Kerim landed on the ground, gently placing her down beside his motorcycle. It was keeled over against the sidewalk, the cement underneath it raised up from the quake.

He waved to someone off in the distance and soon Walid was running up to him.

"Walid, ride the bike and bring Cristal to your home. Take good care of her," Kerim commanded.

Walid nodded his head, his eyes staring at the wings on Kerim's back.

"*Maffoom?* Do you understand me, Walid?"

"Yes, yes. *Maffoom.* I will take care of Mizz Cristal, Kerim."

Walid turned and picked up the motorcycle.

Kerim pulled the keys from his pocket and tossed them at Walid who caught them in his hands. Kerim looked at Cristal, the expression on his face showing his steadfastness and conviction.

"Remember, Cristal, you have untapped powers that not even Raffe knows about. Why would we be sent here to destroy you if this were not true?"

The rational part of her wanted to scream but the new Cristal, the one who wasn't afraid anymore, kept her cool.

"So Harry was right. You were sent to destroy me."

He looked away briefly. "Yes, that is true, but I didn't know that when I met you. My original memories were removed and implanted with temporary human ones. Now that I know you, I cannot and *will not* let anyone harm you. Never doubt that, no matter what," he said, his voice breaking with emotion.

She knew that what he was saying was true.

His gaze shot upward to the sky that seemed to be swallowing the stars. "Now go! There's no time!" he cried out.

He was right. There was no time. She ran over to the motorcycle and jumped on. Walid started the engine. She turned to say goodbye but instead was met with giant silver wings soaring, carrying Kerim into the sky.

She watched as he ascended into the dark clouds, disappearing into the heavens. Kerim Ilgaz, her Guardian with wings.

Gabriel, Harry and now Kerim... all gone in one day. No time to cry or say goodbye.

She placed her arms around Walid's waist, closed her eyes as he revved the engine and pulled the bike out onto the road. She didn't know what was in store or what the future held for her, but one thing was for sure—she was determined to continue Harry's mission to seek the truth.

"Hold on, Mizz Cristal," Walid called back to her. "I am taking you to my home in Megiddo."

"I am not familiar with that town," Cristal replied. "Is it a small village?"

"Oh? But it is famous place," he insisted. "You do know it."

Cristal tilted her head.

"Sorry, Megiddo doesn't ring a bell."

Walid said, "Ah, yes, yes. I forget. You may know it by the Eenglesh name, Armageddon."

Dear Reader,

Find out what happens to Harry, Cristal, and Kerim in "**RESIST**" (book 2 of the Among Us Trilogy). Find out about the status of my writing projects and other fun stuff by registering to the Truth Seeker Book Club at the official Among Us Trilogy website at http://www.amongus.ca.

If you enjoyed "**Doubt**" (book 1 of the Among Us Trilogy), please take a few minutes to submit a review where you purchased the book. As a writer, I appreciate your feedback and your review will help others like you find my work.

I've included Chapter 1 of the next book in the trilogy on the next few pages. For more information about my other books and film projects, visit my blog at http://www.anne-raevasquez.com or send me a tweet @write2film.

Till our paths cross again,

Anne-Rae Vasquez

Truth Seekers unite!

SNEAK PEEK OF RESIST, BOOK 2
OF THE AMONG US TRILOGY

CHAPTER 1
BETWEEN LIFE AND DEATH

Harry stepped through the light, his foot landing on thin air. He keeled forward expecting to hit the ground headfirst but instead he was suspended in a void of emptiness—a dark vacuum.

"Anyone out there?" he asked.

He was met with dead silence. Funny he should think that. Wasn't this what being dead felt like?

Enough. Focus on completing the mission.

He had to find his mother, Cristal's father and bring them back to the land of the living.

"Mom, can you hear me?" he called out.

Nothing but silence. He began to wonder if he had made the right decision to cross over to the spiritual world. What if crossing over meant he had to die doing it?

A sharp pain stabbed his heart. He grabbed his chest until the pain subsided to a dull ache. He was somewhat relieved that he still had a beating heart. Guess he wasn't dead after all.

Maybe time stood still on this side. What if he ended up floating here in spiritual emptiness forever?

"Harry?" his mother's voice entered the void.

"Mom?" he called out. "Mom!"

Twisting his body, he tried to float towards the sound.

Something icy grabbed his arm and yanked him downward. He began free falling into the abysmal blackness.

Should he brace himself for the landing?

Before another thought could enter his mind, his body slammed into a solid surface knocking him out on impact.

❧

WHAT SEEMED LIKE HOURS LATER, but could have been minutes, (Harry wasn't entirely sure) he gained consciousness. He was laying flat on his back. Sounds and voices of people around him and the bleating of car horns jolted him awake.

"Harry!"

The voice sounded so familiar and yet. His eyes were trying to adjust to the bright light.

"Thank God! It is you, Harry."

Harry felt someone pull himself into a sitting position.

"Are you okay?"

He glanced up to see who the Good Samaritan was but instead, he was staring dumbfounded at the lopsided grin of someone he didn't expect to ever see again.

"Harry! I'm so glad I found you! I thought I was going crazy!"

"Gabriel?"

"I don't know what happened. I was rushing towards you and Kerim and then you all disappeared."

Harry racked his brain to comprehend what was happening. He, along with Cristal and the others, had watched Gabriel get shot in the back and die on the street. But here was Gabriel in the flesh right in front of him. He reached out to touch Gabriel's arm half expecting to feel nothingness. Surely, he must be hallucinating.

"I've been trying to find the others but nobody here has seen them," Gabriel said. "Here, let me help you up."

Gabriel grabbed a hold of Harry's arm and put it over his shoulder, easing him up to his feet.

Harry took a deep breath. The salty sea air mixed with the smell of diesel smoke spewing from the tailpipes of cars driving by filled his lungs.

Wait a minute. Where am I?

He looked around, checking his surroundings.

It was incredible. They were standing in the same spot where Yaffa and her security thugs had shot Gabriel down.

He glanced around, feeling disoriented. The sun was setting against the turquoise blue sky. The streets were busy with young men smoking *sheesha* water pipes, laughing and horsing around on the beach. This was not what Harry had expected to see in Limbo or Purgatory or whatever this place was.

"Harry, you look like you've seen a ghost," Gabriel said.

Harry swallowed hard and forced a smile.

Doesn't he remember getting killed?

Harry's Truth Seeker skills kicked in. He did not know what would happen if he told Gabriel the cold hard facts. Better go along with the situation until he can figure out what is happening.

"I am not feeling well. Why don't we go find a place to talk?" Harry said.

"Sure thing. We can get you something to eat."

Harry let Gabriel walk ahead while he scanned landmarks around him, making note of the location of where the portal would have been on the "other side". It was the place where the walls of Akko used to stand before they crumbled into dust during the earthquake. Here on this side of reality, instead of walls there stood sixty-foot high steel bars.

If I'm going to get back to the other side, I have to come back to this spot.

"Harry, c'mon. The others will be relieved to see you."

Others?

"Uh, Gabriel. What others?" Harry asked but Gabriel had darted ahead.

He followed Gabriel into the small shop. It was a typical fast food restaurant in the area. Sharp smells of spices and greasy food hit his nostrils while the sound of Arabic pop music blasted from a boom box sitting on a shelf behind the front counter. Groups of young people sat at the wooden tables spread across the room. A number of the guys glanced up, eyeing him suspiciously as he walked past.

Gabriel waved to someone sitting at a table in the back of the shop.

"Look who I've found!"

As he walked closer, Harry could see two people sitting across from each other at the table. One was a woman with her back to him and the other was a middle-aged man with Latino features, olive complexion, dark wavy hair, and a pointed nose.

When they reached the table, the woman stood up and turned to face him. Harry's heart started racing when their eyes met.

"Mom?"

It had been a year since he last saw his mother Bina. She was thinner; her hair was greyer and the wrinkles around her eyes deeper than he remembered.

Waves of emotion ran through him. Every cell in his body wanted to run to her and hug her just as he did when he was a terrified six-year-old child lost in a crowded shopping mall.

The look of concern on her face and the way she glanced over her shoulder forced him to realize that this was not the time or the place. The reunion celebration would have to wait until their safety was established.

"Harry, we need to be discreet," she said in a hushed voice. "Sit down beside me and face Roberto."

She motioned with her hand towards the man sitting across from her. Roberto lifted his chin slightly in acknowledgement.

Gabriel asked, "So you know Rose?"

Harry shot a glance at his mother. Was *Rose* her alias?

Harry's mother turned to Gabriel.

"Please keep your voice down and take a seat."

Gabriel took the chair beside Roberto while Harry sat down beside her. There were many questions he wanted to ask but he remained quiet. The answers will come, all in good time.

The loud music and the noise from the different conversations in the room decreased in volume. Harry checked over his shoulder to see that all eyes were on them.

Roberto lowered his voice, speaking with a subtle Spanish accent, "Harry, your mother Bina has taken the alias *Rose* and you must refer to her as this until we get out of here."

Gabriel's eyebrows shot up and his mouth opened as if to say something.

Harry pulled his focus back on Roberto.

"I'm assuming that Roberto is not your real name either," Harry said.

"Correct. I'm Carlos Hernandez. Cristal's father."

BEFORE YOU GO...

I hope you enjoyed reading the excerpt of RESIST, book 2. As a thank you, I'm giving away a free book in hopes that you will check out more of my work. All you have to do is register your email address to the Truth Seekers Book Club.

Click here to receive a special bonus book!

ACKNOWLEDGMENTS

A huge thank you to my Truth Seekers for their contributions and participation in Harry Doubt's missions. I've listed my beta readers who participated in my Truth Seeker missions and helped me shape the characters in Doubt. I couldn't have done it without their enthusiastic help. If you visit www.amongus.ca , go to the *Characters* link in the top menu and check out all the fun and collaborative missions we did together.

Josefina Rosado as Cristal Hernandez (alias Mist)

Anne-Rae Vasquez as Harry Doubt (alias Zero)

Jeanne Lee as Joanna Chan (alias Onyx)

Khaled Talib, author of Smokescreen as Rinaldo Ricci (alias Red Fox)

Donna Bonastella as Angelica Martinelli (alias Venus)

Macqueline Cajandab as Serena Keensky (alias Lioness)

Josefina Rosado, Anne-Rae Vasquez as Kerim Ilgaz (alias Shadow)

Kathleen McMahon as Jenna Adams (alias Celestial Nymph)

LIST OF CHARACTERS

Harry Doubt (alias Zero) – 24 year old former child prodigy; Operations Manager for Global Nation by day; by night he is trying to find out why his mother and other parents of child prodigies were kidnapped by Global Nation in the Middle East. He is the programmer who designed and created "Truth Seekers", a popular online virtual reality game with over a million players. Changed his last name from "Doub" to "Doubt" after his father passed away stating that he was never really a father to him anyway; has dual Israeli and American citizenship.

Cristal Hernandez (alias Mist) – 24 year old former child prodigy, graduated from Global Nation University with Harry Doubt at 19 years with a PhD in Computer Science, not religious but had a Catholic upbringing; book smart but doubts herself; just realized she has special powers and is learning to control them. This character was inspired by Josefina Rosado.

Serena Keensky (alias Lioness) – athletic, teaches self defense at Global Nation, has a black belt in several forms of martial arts including Krav Maga; is an avid Truth Seeker gamer; lived in many places around the world, the last being in the Philippines where her father is the ambassador for Russia; is a no-nonsense person. This character was inspired by Macqueline Cajandab

Gabriel Windam (alias Graphix) – top player of the Truth Seekers online virtual reality game; loves the 70's era; loyal to Harry.

Kerim Ilgaz – was hired to provide Security to GN by Harry; served in the Turkish army for four years prior to that.

Raffe (aka Archangel Rafael) – when in human form is an abrasive, tough Israeli; in angelic form is a formidable power; has a strange sense of humor.

Aaron Doub – Harry's father, famous GN Physicist who died right before he was able to prove the theory of time travel; was never close to his son; loved his wife Bina but always put his work ahead of his family; has Israeli and American citizenship.

Joanna Chan (alias Onyx) – IT support at Global Nation, a charitable organization. She takes her online gaming seriously. She has the most weapons and treasures in the alternate reality game called Truth Seekers. She appears quiet and naive but her looks are deceiving. This character was inspired by Jeanne L.

Bina Schwartz – Harry's mother; Israeli wife and mother; denied her spirituality.

Saeed Nariman – GN Physicist and assistant to Aaron Doub; Bina and Harry's confidante and friend.

Shelley Lionheart – president of Global Nation University and charitable organization with headquarters around the world.

ABOUT THE AUTHOR

Anne-Rae Vasquez latest novel Reveal, book 3 of the Among Us Trilogy was released in May 2018. Her previous novels, _RESIST,_ book 2 of the Among Us Trilogy and _Imminent_-a Truth Seeker Conspiracy Thriller were released in November 2014. _Doubt_, Book 1 of the Among Us Trilogy was a Gold winner in the Readers' Favorite Book Awards 2014.

Her debut novel Almost a Turkish Soap Opera was adapted into a screenplay and later produced into an award winning feature film and web series and was her directorial debut. Her other works include: Gathering Dust - a collection of poems, Salha's Secrets to Middle Eastern Cooking Cookbook published by AR Publishing Inc. and Teach Yourself Great Web Design in a Week, published by Sams.net (a division of Macmillan Publishing).

In her parallel life, she hosts/produces Fiction Frenzy TV, a weekly VLog channel featuring indie artists, authors, filmmakers and musicians. In addition to this, she freelances as a journalist for Blasting News (and formerly Digital Journal) and manages a film production company.

www.ingramcontent.com/pod-product-compliance
Lightning Source LLC
Chambersburg PA
CBHW060435180626
46817CB00007B/2827